$25
7/14 F

Assassination of Light

Assassination of Light

Modern Saudi Short Stories

Edited and Translated by
Abu Bakr Bagader
and
Ava Molnar Heinrichsdorff

An Original by Three Continents Press

©Abu Bakr A. Bagader 1990 and
Ava Molnar Heinrichsdorff 1990

First English-language edition

Three Continents Press
1901 Pennsylvania Avenue
Suite 407
Washington, D.C. 20009

Library of Congress Cataloging-in-publication Data:

Assassination of Light: Modern Saudi Short Stories/edited
and translated by Abu Bakr Bagader and Ava Molnar
Heinrichsdorff.
    p.   cm.
ISBN 0-89410-598-1. --ISBN 0-89410-599-X (pbk.)
    1. Short stories, Arabic--Saudi arabia--Translations into
English. 2. Short stories, Arabic--20th century-- Translations
into English. 3. Short stories, English--Translations from Arabic.
I. Bagader, Abu Bakr. II. Heinrichsdorff, Ava Molnar.
PJ8005.82.E5A87 1990
892'.730108--dc20
                                                            89-20596
                                                                CIP

©Cover Design by Three Continents of art
by Max K. Winkler 1990

Everything Is an Empty Repetition Without Meaning

For Othman Brian Llewellyn

Contents

Preface by Abu Bakr A. Bagader

When I began preparing this collection of short stories, I gathered almost all the contemporary short fiction published in Saudi Arabia. In reading through the stories, I recognized two major groups: the concerns, themes and styles of the "old" writers, and those of the "young."

The main feature of the older generation's writings is a "social" or "corporate" perspective, portraying individuals in a distinctively culture-specific society, a Muslim and Middle Eastern one. These writers play the traditional role of the Arab poet in representing the voices of content and discontent with the social issues facing their changing society.

The younger writers differ in both theme and style. They stress more individualistic concerns of alienation, stress and tension. They experiment creatively in their use of language, and sometimes draw upon western techniques of short story writing.

In this volume I have chosen mostly from the older group, hoping to collect a representative anthology of the younger writers in a future volume. As a student of the social sciences, I find the concerns of these older writers closer to my own. While they dramatize social discontent and voice objections, rejection, and quests for change, their approaches are never radical. They present an image of a changing society that is at once nostalgic about its past and eager to evolve. They address issues of male-female relations, the rural-urban dichotomy, patriarchal authority, and more. From them a reader can construct a realistic socio-cultural picture of Saudi Arabia.

Their arrangement emphasizes this. The first six stories stress the nostalgia. They represent the "old types" satirically, ironically or humorously to dramatize the depth of the "old" psychology and its

1

incompatablity with modernity.

The next five deal with women's issues—clearly the most popular topic in Westerners' writings (or questions) about Saudi Arabia. The writers, both women and men, show us many of Arabia's pitfalls and prejudices; they show the need for self-criticism and reform in the status and roles of women. However, they do not propose that Arabia merely ape the trends of other societies. Their quest is for evolution from within, for change that will correct injustice and abuse without abandoning the society's morals and values.

The last five stories dramatize the complex effects of socio-cultural change in customs and technological development.

Of course, it is futile to justify one's choices of artistic materials in purely rational terms, so I will not discard the factor of personal taste. I chose stories that appealed to me. I hope that readers will come to these stories with a variety of motives, from literary to anthropological, political to sociological, and that all will find them interesting. I hope, too, that the collection will offer a richer view of Saudi Arabia than the stereotypical "oil-rich, conservative, traditional, tribal" caricature.

I greatly appreciate the assistance given to me by the Jeddah Literary Society. Finally, I would like to thank Ava Molnar Heinrich-sdorff for daring to get involved with this adventure of presenting foreign literature to western readers. I appreciate her discriminating literary sense and immense writing talent. She reshaped the stories into meaningful English texts and clarified aspects that might "go without saying" to Saudi Arabian readers, while preserving each author's intent.

Abu Bakr A. Bagader
Jeddah, 1988

Preface by Ava Molnar Heinrichsdorff

Improbably, as a Hungarian-born American, I became involved in *Assassination of Light* in the best Arabic fashion—through connections. My son, a landscape architect in Mecca, knew that his good friend, Dr. Abu Bakr A. Bagader, needed someone to work on his rough translations of these stories. They asked me if I would undertake the project. At first I was curious, and then, when I had read the manuscripts, I was enthusiastic.

I found the stories fascinating both as tales that deserve to be read and as dramatizations of how it is, how it feels, to live in a culture that in less than forty years has accomplished two or three hundred "European years" of change. In this rapidly-changing culture, the "generation gap" between parent and child is the gap of a century.

As one would expect, these Saudi Arabian authors view their cultural transformation with hope, dread or nostalgia. They give us anachronism, irony, lyricism, satire, humor and pathos. And passion.

Some are "genre" stories, vignettes of traditional village life. Some are comic, such as "Auntie Ruqayyah's News" and "The Bad-Tempered Man." Two are tales of dragon-mothers—"Ali the Teacher" and "By My Satisfaction With You"—which inevitably make us Westerners aware of the limited extent of authority available to "sheltered" women, and their consequent temptation to abuse these small powers. (Perhaps that is why Chinese literature, too, is so rich in dragon-mothers.) "Abu Rayhan, the Water Carrier" is an archetypal "tragic clown," and Zahra in "The Secret and the Death" is an archetypal "wise fool." She is also a sacrificial hero, reminiscent of Hester Prynne in *The Scarlet Letter*.

3

Five stories examine women's roles. The first girls' school in Saudi Arabia opened in 1967 and, already, there are women doctors, dentists, educators, lawyers (my Arab daughter-in-law, for instance). It is no surprise, then, that some of these stories protest the victimization of women when "protection" is corrupted to exploitation, as in "Poor, Oh! Chastity!" and "A Woman for Sale." (Both of these were written by men, from a female protagonist's point of view. It interests me that both men and women are writing "feminist" fiction.)

"The Assassination of Light at the River's Flow" shows us one of these new schoolgirls who has been exposed, even within the sheltering walls of her academy, to a glimpse of other possibilities—just enough to change her expectations, so that her parents' best efforts on her behalf turn sour and then violent. "My Hair Grew Long Again" demonstrates the "modern" expectations of intelligent young women who crave, like Nora in Ibsen's *A Doll House*, to be adults in their marriages and in their society—not merely pampered pets, however cherished they might be. (Both of these stories were written by women.)

"Violets," by contrast, is a tender story that reconciles tradition and innovation, loyalty and individuality, duty and compassion—through a combination of patience, trust, and a karma or fate that just happens to be, for once, capriciously benign. Because the story guarantees nothing, and is *not* a simplistic or didactic "virtue-will-always-be-rewarded" parable, we are immensely relieved that *some* people might find serenity and balance amid the cultural turmoil.

Several stories focus on technological revolution and its attendant social disruption. "Sa'id the Searcher" is at one extreme in its romantic nostalgia for a better, nobler past. So is "The Last Poet," a dystopian satire of what is to come, if Saudi Arabia doesn't modify its obsession with materialism and glittering gadgetry. "Rite of Passage," on the other hand, shows how tradition, though vital to the lives of those who cherish its meanings, is reduced to tragic barbarism when its meanings are lost. In the bitterly ironic "Homecoming" a young man comprehends neither his new world nor his old world well enough to attain his dream; and in "Tell Us a Story, Abu Auf" (another "wise fool" story) we get a painful glimpse of both sides, weighted toward the older, better days.

Every culture must continually balance tradition and innovation if it is to survive. If it encrusts itself in inflexible tradition, the young abandon it, and it dies; if it abruptly loses all faith in its traditions, its people lose their identity and confidence, and it dies. Saudi Arabia, fortunate in having more choices than many other fast-developing nations, is particularly self-aware in its struggle toward balance.

Yet, although a fair amount of Middle Eastern literature is finding

4

its way to the Western world, we have had very few works from the Kingdom of Saudi Arabia. The most conservative yet one of the most advantaged of Middle Eastern nations, the most exclusive yet the most multi-cultural, Saudi Arabia is, in many ways, the most interesting. It is paradoxical, dynamic and, above all, "literary."

Ava Molnar Heinrichsdorff
Colorado Springs, 1988

Auntie Ruqayyah's News

by Muhammad Ali Rida Quddus

Ruqayyah, or Auntie Ruqayyah as the neighbors called her, loved to sit comfortably on her satin sofa in her traditional *raushan* window, leaning against her damask pillows. She was fortunate that her *raushan* overlooked the main *suq*, and that the lantern of the *kabab al-miro* vendor lit the stage of this, her theater. The stage was peopled by the sellers of the traditional dishes that Auntie Ruqayyah's nose appreciated—*fava beans, maqliyyah, sambusa, mutabbaq,* and more—and their customers, and the neighbors in their goings and comings.

Fatima, her maid, brought her all the gossip she could glean, both the important and the trivial. Fatima knew that she had better have some news each time she saw her mistress, and sometimes she hoarded an item against a dull day if she thought it might keep for a few hours without spoiling. Auntie Ruqayyah needed a constant supply to fuel her social conversation. Her social life.

As time passed in practice, Auntie Ruqayyah's powers of observation and deduction became very sharp indeed. She could read people's lives from their faces. She would settle her heavy body in the *raushan* and observe, marking whether anyone behaved in any unusual way. If someone was late, for instance, she began her calculations. She knew that Amm Ahmad always opened his *kabab al-Miro* stall just before sunset, when Sadaqah returned from his store in the food market, so she could always tell if Sadaqah was late, for Uncle Ahmed was as punctual as the official clock—and whenever there was such a change in someone's timing, Auntie Ruqayyah would worry until her talents for observation and imagination found interesting excuses for them. These became essential materials for the news with which she would entertain her friends and visitors. Of course, she never forgot to

7

end her report with: "All this in confidence, mind you. One must be discreet and compassionate, and I mentioned it only because of my concern, and my trust in you."

One day Auntie Ruqayyah noticed that Salih, the husband of her neighbor Ratibah, was late going home. Surely there was conflict in the household. Fatimah had mentioned that Salih and Ratibah sometimes fought. What caused them to fight? There had to be a sin or a sorrow.

When Fatimah was pouring Turkish coffee for Auntie Ruqayyah she dropped a news item that stopped the coffee cup halfway between table and lip. "Ratibah and Salih must have had a fight," she reported. "Ratibah has gone to her parents' home with the children."

That was an authentic piece of news! Fatimah had had it from a dependable source, a relative of Ratibah's.

"Well, what else?" Auntie Ruqayyah urged.

"That's all I know."

Auntie Ruqayyah sipped her coffee meditatively and then asked, "But my daughter, what caused their problem? What was the trouble?"

"I don't know, Mistress."

"Truly you are a useless fool!" she exploded. "What's the point, if you don't know the cause? You're good for nothing! How can you be so superficial?"

"My Auntie Ruqayyah, I could not wait to find out more. I was afraid of being late for your coffee."

"May Allah punish you! Is coffee more important than Ratibah's marriage? Do you think I can't make a cup of coffee myself?"

"Do not worry," Fatimah reassured her. "I'll get you the details, as many as I can, when . . ."

"Look!" Auntie Ruqayyah leaned toward the window, peering intently at the street. Curiosity moved Fatimah, so she looked over Auntie Ruqayyah's shoulder, but she saw nothing that deserved attention.

"Look, oh girl Fatimah!"

"I am looking, but I do not see anything special."

"Is that not Salih?"

"It looks like him—yes, it is."

"And he is with a woman!" The woman was talking to him animatedly, and he was answering her with a smile, and she was nodding and talking, and he was looking down at her and responding. "Who can it be?"

"Not his wife, that is certain."

"His mother, perhaps?" The woman was wearing a dark blue veil,

8

and she didn't think Khadijah had one like that, unless it was new.

"No, my mistress, that is not Khadijah."

"Everyone speaks of Salih as a good, religious man," she speculated. "If he talks to a woman in the middle of the street in front of the whole neighborhood, he must have a legal relationship with her, or he would be ashamed. So who is she, then?"

No doubt that woman was the point of conflict between Salih and Ratibah! Salih must have married her! He must have taken a second wife!

She considered other possibilities as Fatimah removed the coffee service, but they were all weak by comparison. Auntie Ruqayyah always dismissed weak possibilities. Had she known the truth, that the woman was merely asking directions to the coppersmith's shop, she would have found it entirely unsatisfactory, so perhaps it was just as well that she didn't know.

As she studied the question, her close friend Nafisah entered, politely clapping her hands to signal her presence.

"Welcome, welcome, thanks for coming, my house is lightened by your presence, my friend Nafusah!" she exclaimed in her customary greeting. "Nafusah" was an affectionate nickname. She beckoned her guest to her side on the sofa to let her see the street with its sellers' cries and playing children's shouts. "How are you, Nafusah, and how have you spent your days and nights? How are your children?" She clapped her hands for Fatimah. "Oh girl, Fatmah, come and serve us some black-eyed peas or *manfush* from the *suq!*"

Nafisah laughed until her gold teeth showed. "You're never bored with watching the street, are you?"

"Ah!" she sighed. "I'm lonely, oh Nafusah. Since my girls were married and my husband died, all I have, as you see, is this *raushan* and this watching."

Nafisah sought to comfort her. "Actually, it is a sweet amusement."

"Do not forget," added Auntie Ruqayyah with the emphasis of mystery, "I see things that others do not see."

"What have you seen, my friend?" Tell me!"

She started in with her enthusiastic preamble. "I never want to say anything about other people's lives, you know. But these are the facts, and may Allah forgive me! I was so suprised!"

"What happened, Ruqayyah?"

"By Allah, then, let this be secret between us!"

"Do not be afraid, my sister. Your secret will be in a deep

well."

The appetizer was a success, so Ruqayyah served the entree. "This morning I saw Salih in the *suq* with a strange woman. And some days ago I knew that Ratibah had returned to her family's house."

"Why? What has happened between them, do you think?"

"I do not know, sister. Ratibah is a jewel of a wife. But what can you say of men? Their eyes are always empty."

"Do not say that, Ruqayyah! Salih is a very religious man. Everybody says he is a good man."

"You see how appearances deceive? With my own eyes I saw him, from this very *raushan*. But by the names of Allah, do not tell anyone what I have told you!" She leaned toward Nafisah and whispered, "I mentioned it only because you are my faithful friend, my best friend. But it is not our right to interfere in others' affairs. It has been said that he who enters between the onion's layers will get nothing but their bad smell."

"Have no concern. But who would believe that Salih would do that to poor Ratibah? Oh, my friend, men are like that indeed. Good for nothing." Then she explained her speculations, which became more interesting with every sentence.

When Nafisah took her leave she walked directly to another neighbor's house to tell her the news, confidentially, of course. Thus the story was told from neighbor to neighbor, from mouth to ear, and by afternoon when it reached Khadijah, the mother of Salih, it went like this:

Salih and Ratibah had been fighting a great deal of late, because Salih was threatening to take another wife. This very morning, when he told her that he had already become engaged, she objected strenuously to his shameful deed, and declared that she would divorce him. Then he beat her, and swore he would never free her from their marriage.

But nobody knew where the news came from. All just said, "Everybody knows it!"

Despite her arthritis, Khadija ran to her son's house. There, to her surprise, she found her daughter-in-law Ratibah taking tea with her mother. She was even more surprised to see them both in a very happy mood. There were no apparent bruises. There was no apparent anger.

"Are you all right, Umm Khadija?" Ratibah asked her.

"Fine," she answered shortly. She was confused and irritated. After two cups of tea she was able to ask, "Has anything happened between you and Salih?"

Ratibah and her mother laughed and laughed, and Khadijah's discomfort returned, bringing humiliation with it.

10

"So even you heard the story," Ratibah finally said.

"Story?"

"Is there anything hidden? Three days ago when Salih was out of town I went to my mother's house for a visit. And that was enough for people who have nothing but other people's lives to preoccupy their interest. They started a story that grew. Is that what brought you here, Umm Khadija?" And Ratibah's mother laughed the coughing laugh of old people, and Khadijah laughed too.

The next day when she was visiting her friends, Khadijah dropped in on Auntie Ruqayyah. For quite a while they commiserated together about the way gossip spreads and grows, like weeds, like tumors.

"I never want to say anything about other people's lives, as you know," Auntie Ruqayyah said self-righteously. "One has no right to interfere in others' affairs. He who enters between the onion's layers will get nothing but their bad smell, you know." But before they had drunk their third cup of tea Khadijah had learned from Auntie Ruqayyah that Nafisah had been to the dentist in Jeddah, and that she was going to get more of her teeth crowned, but this time it would not be with gold. It would be with something more expensive, something white, something new, and it would resemble the natural teeth of youth so closely that no one would be able to know they were not real. Every day something new was invented to restore youth to ageing women, and soon, if women had no dignity, no one would be able to tell the mothers from the daughters.

"All this in confidence, mind you. One must be discreet and compassionate. I mention it only because of my concern for her, and my trust in you."

The Bad-Tempered Man

by Muhammad Ali Maghribi

There was once a very bad-tempered man who seemed always angry and difficult to deal with. He complained continually. He was at his worst at home, where he saw no need to control his peevishness and choler. His wife was a very patient woman, who appeared obedient to the husband that her fate had given her, though he found disobedience in whatever she did. She had a son and two daughters from him, and she and the children strove to avoid exciting him and igniting his rage.

Once the man became sick and went to his physician, who asked for a urine sample to be collected upon awakening the next morning. He went home with the specimen jar hidden in his pocket, angry with these new doctors. What could be the connection between his painful legs and his urine? He continued to fret against modern doctoring until the next day when he took the full specimen jar, again hidden in his pocket, to the laboratory. The technician just took it and told him to return the next day for the lab report.

He went home agitated by all these ridiculous delays. What was the use of all those years of schooling that doctors had these days, if they could no longer just examine, diagnose and prescribe, as doctors always used to do? These days they wouldn't say the first word without lab reports on urine, or blood, or X-rays, or some nonsense.

The next morning he returned to the lab, got the report, and took it to the doctor's office. The waiting room was full of patients and it was a long, tedious hour before he was finally called.

When the doctor opened the envelope and read the lab report, surprise appeared in his eyes, and he smiled. Reassured, the man also smiled eagerly, awaiting the decision; had he not been known for dignified respectablity, he might have laughed out loud. But before the

12

doctor could open his mouth, the telephone rang. "Could that machine have no better timing than to ring right now?" our friend mumbled impatiently. "Couldn't that caller have waited until my appointment was finished?" But the call involved an emergency, and the doctor began to put things in his bag while telling our friend, with a soft laugh, that the urine test would have to be repeated.

What! Was it not enough to waste two days before a diagnosis and cure? Must he now waste two more? But before he could complain the doctor added, "There is something wrong, I am sure. The tests indicate pregnancy."

The words fell upon his head like a storm. The physician left the clinic to go wherever he was wanted, and our friend, unconscious of what surrounded him, unaware of how long he remained in the clinic, finally somehow found his way toward his home. His face blushed, his breath panted, the world spun in his mind; he didn't know he was walking. If only he might be buried! It would be better than such a shame. The doctor knew. The lab technicians all knew. Pregnancy! He had recently heard of transexuals, men who had turned into women. He felt seventy, or eighty. When he entered his house his legs could no longer carry him and he fell on the floor. His eyes were burning and his throat was dry.

"What is the matter?" his wife asked in surprise.

But he looked at her rudely and shouted, "Get out of my sight and don't ask me stupid questions! Don't ever ask me about anything!" She went to the kitchen, and he lay down on the cushions in his private room. What a crisis, what a shameful crisis! He looked down on his big stomach and his swollen legs, and he wept. It was not his nature to weep, but the tears came out of his eyes against his will. The injustice of it! Why should he, the straight, good man, whose life was divided between his house and his store, his store and the grand mosque, the grand mosque and his house, suffer such an affliction?

His wife bought the dishes for dinner, but he waved them away. He could not look at them, or at her. When she tried to urge him to eat he shouted, "I told you, I don't want to eat anything! Don't try to tell me what I want! What I want is to be left in peace!" He lay there all night, unable to move, unable to sleep.

After he had refused to take his usual breakfast with his family, and the children had left for their schools, his wife decided to risk his temper. He didn't see her approach him; he was lying with his face to the wall, weeping.

"Are you crying, Abu Muhammad?" she asked in a voice he was not used to, for she was beginning to wonder whether this was indeed more than one of his normal petulances over some trifle, the sort that he

13

sometimes atoned for with awkwardly given gifts or compliments. "I have never seen you cry before. What is it that causes you such grief?" She began to wipe his tears and stroke his hair. "I'm your wife, the mother of your children—why do you not tell me of your troubles? Please, Abu Muhammad, tell me. Nobody will ever know your secret. I'm the person closest to you, so please, do not hide anything from me."

He looked at her with weakness and failure apparent upon him and sighed a deep, long sigh that told his despair. Finally she persuaded him to speak. "It is the disintegration of our times," he groaned. "Oh, Mother of Muhammad, I wish that Allah had taken my soul before this came upon me!"

"May Allah, the compassionate, the merciful, protect you!" exclaimed his wife. "*What* has come upon you? Tell me, that I may understand!"

"Better that you not understand."

"I must understand, whatever it is," she insisted.

Abu Muhammad gave her a long look. "I went to the doctor yesterday," he said, "carrying the results of the tests. . ." Then his shivering voice was stopped by his sobbing.

"The tests!" she exclaimed. "What did he say?"

"He said. . .the tests show signs. . .signs. . .signs. . .of. . ."

"*Pregnancy?*"

He sat up and stared at her. "Who told you that? Who told you? That doctor!"

She laughed. "Nobody told me; I just. . ."

But before she could explain, he shouted, "Are you laughing at me? Are you laughing at my calamity? Does my shame amuse you? You. . ."

"Do not be anxious, Abu Muhammad," she interrupted, still laughing. "I was cleaning the bathroom and the sample jar fell down, spilling some of your urine. So I filled it with mine, and it must. . ."

"Why did you do that? How could you. . ."

"Afraid of your temper. I knew that if you came in and saw what had happened you would rage around, and shout, and curse us, and call us *Ya Mala'een, Ya Kelab*. So I tried to protect us. I often have to do that, you know. I just refilled your jar with my own urine." To his silence she added, "You are telling me that I am pregnant. I wasn't sure. Be happy! That's good news!"

14

Ali, the Teacher

by *Fouad Abd al-Hamid Anqawi*

Everything about him singles him out, because neither years nor events can change him. The pallor of his face, as if he were malnourished or had some chronic disease; the old clothes, clean but stained with time and use, that announce his displeasure in newness; the once-blue coat that imitates the gray of clouds; the old dust-dyed turban. The slightly hunchbacked teacher Ali walks briskly to school, or home from school, always carrying books. He greets everyone with a smile, but without stopping to waste time over nonsense or "unimportant questions," as he calls them. Ali is accurate as a calculator. He walks with fixed discipline that is shaped by hours, minutes and even seconds. He sleeps and eats by the clock, and enters the school long before the earliest student.

"Discipline, discipline," he exhorts his students before the morning greetings. He likes discipline in behavior, in notebooks, in the orderly placement of pencils. Ali loves symmetry. His teaching style is firm, knowledgeable and patient; he tries every means of making the boys understand their lessons. Administrators, school inspectors and fellow teachers respect him, even though he refuses to participate in the extracurricular activities or picnics.

Teacher Ali lives in Mecca, in an old house that his mother inherited from her father. When Ali's father died, his mother asked Ali to live with her, and insisted until he consented. He will not have her angry with him.

Ali has a few good friends, especially Shaykh Salih, grocer and gravemaker. Often they walk to the holy Grand Mosque together to pray their sunset and evening prayers.

It grieved Shaykh Salih, who was the father of many children, that

Ali was ageing in loneliness. "I had a dream last night," Shaykh Salih said one evening.

"I hope something good," replied Ali.

"I dreamt that you were walking among a big crowd, putting on white clothes—and there was singing, and drums were playing."

Ali was quiet for a while and then said, "It is either death or. . ."

"Or a wedding party."

"It makes no difference whether it is in this life or in the hereafter, and the hereafter is eternal," said Ali.

"This life is pleasure, and the best of pleasures is a righteous, faithful woman," said Shaykh Salih.

"A righteous woman, oh! Where is such a one? Our age is an age of wonders, and whence come wonders but from women!"

"You have no experience. A man's life without a wife is a lost life. Also, marriage is half a man's religion."

"Enough!" said Ali. "Shaykh Salih, you know enough of my personal life!" He stood up to leave, and on the way home began to think of the remaining two months before exams. Suddenly his heart beat faster. Two months only! Oh, Allah! He wondered whether Hassan, son of the deceased Yaqub, would want special tutoring again. Would Ali consent? He would be very pressured in those two months. He did not enjoy tutoring this rather dumb boy and his sister, but had consented last year because of their mother's friendship with his mother. His mother had insisted.

The mother of those children; it started an echo in him. That polite, gentle woman. He had seen her face only once, a quick glimpse. He did not recognize her well, but for her full body, her tall figure, that told him she was middle-aged, patient, strong. She had dignity. She spent her limited earnings as a seamstress on her children, too proud to ask any of her relatives for help. "A woman of that type, or nothing," the hidden echo said. He had refused to take payment for the lessons, but she had spoken from behind the door: "We know that what we offer is very little, but our ambitions are high and our means are small. We do not know how else to thank you, so please accept this small amount." He had admired her, and refused. Her voice now echoed in his ears and he tried to picture the face he had not seen but for that quick moment.

In correcting student papers he lost those orphan memories, and her blurred face vanished like a rainbow on a dreamy day.

A few evenings later, when Ali had put off his coat and *thaub* and hung his timeless turban on its hanger, his mother requested, "Ali, put them on again and go to the market to buy us a delicious dinner. A dear guest has come to visit us." Then she added shyly, "Please bring *mutabbaq*, my dear son! Umm Hassan visits us so rarely, I've asked her to have dinner with us. She would like to talk to you about something very important."

Many pictures sprang before his eyes again and he found himself descending energetically, not caring how his evening routine would be disorganized. He returned with the dinner in trembling hands and felt his shivering hands responding to his heart. What could be important to her, but tutoring for that stupid Hassan and his sister? His mother thanked him for bringing the food so quickly.

The women's dinner took a very long time. Why could his mother not put the "important matter" before the food? She was always like that. Food was more important than anything else.

Finally, when Umm Hassan's animated face appeared through the door talking in her feminine way, he could scarcely listen. It was, of course, about the tutoring. He was focused on her face, her black hair, her full body.

His mother interrupted: "But the girl is old enough this year, Umm Hassan. How will Ali be able to see her? This is not permissible."

"Teacher Ali is not a stranger, Umm Ali," said Umm Hassan. "He is like their father. I trust him completely, for he is not only your son, but a very well-behaved and God-fearing gentleman. And her brother Hassan will be with them." Umm Ali laughed in agreement, and Ali was delighted to hear these compliments from Umm Hassan. He wished he could have thanked her, and even told her how he admired her.

"Do you agree, teacher Ali?" she suddenly asked and, before he could respond, went on: "We will expect you tomorrow afternoon, then!" as if she had decided the matter.

When he lay in bed and imagined her, the picture was now clear. He actually thanked himself for his courage to allow himself to visualize not only her face, but whatever of her body the open door had revealed. White face. Thin nose, a little bit flat. Large mouth, with full lips, teeth with glints of gold. Black wavy hair, gathered in a thick loose braid over one shoulder. Confident, strong low voice. The green dress. Full breasts and hips. . .

What did I say? he wondered. What did I intend to say? Where was my resistance, my refusal? Did I accept though I have a very full schedule? No, no, it is not so full. I can manage it. I promised I would.

He wondered at his confusion, and started reorganizing his schedule in his mind.

17

When he knocked on the door Hassan met him with a friendly, stupid smile. Then he heard feminine footsteps approaching and thought how the sister must have matured since last year. He was surprised when he saw Umm Hassan standing before him with a white fringed shawl across her body. It made her beautiful. She took his hand saying, "Hello, welcome, teacher Ali!" After the handshake, he looked at his virgin palm which had never before touched female flesh. He nodded his head and mumbled something, and looked toward the table where they would work. But the girl was waiting there, looking at him. Her body had grown taller and more feminine. Confused, he looked right and left, felt himself sweating and his heart beating, and hurried to seat himself at the table. The most complex mathematical equations would not resolve his confusion.

As he opened a mathematics book he saw Umm Hassan depart, all the time watching him with a paling look as if she were attacking his castle. He cleared his throat and fixed the girl with his sternest scowl, the one that always frightened his pupils, so she looked down into her book; then he told Hassan to begin reading the first problem, and soon they were busy with the drills.

He lagged at the door for a moment as he left, but he did not see her. He reviewed the day's events moment by moment in anxiety. Late that night he got up in the darkness and went to his mother.

"What's the matter?"

"Mother, what is Umm Hassan's name?"

She looked at him with a frown that contracted her whole face. "You're asking me her name in the middle of the night? Why couldn't you wait until morning? Are you all right, Ali? Did you have a nightmare?"

"Mother, please..."

"Saadiyyah, then! Her name is Saadiyyah. Go to sleep!"

He went to bed mumbling "Saadiyya, Saadiyyah," and slept like someone whose long thirst had been quenched. But his mother did not sleep. Ali does not hide his secrets from me, she thought. Where does that poor docile boy get secrets? Is it possible that. . .Oh, no. Impossible.

Strange deviations from routine marked the next week of Ali's life. He did not do what he wanted. One day he surprised his pupils by being unprepared: he had not marked yesterday's papers. Another day he was almost late, and for two hours he couldn't find his glasses.

When he sat on the "confession chair" in front of Shaykh Salih, Shaykh Salih's words fell from his mouth as cool as snow. "I will cut off my right hand," he said, "if there is not a woman in your life."

Teacher Ali couldn't answer. He looked down with a blush, the way a young virgin girl faces her father's announcement of her engagement in front of the whole family. A blush of agreement.

Shaykh Salih realized Ali's anxiety and sat silent for some time. Then he said, "Every knot has a solution. Allah dictates our destinies, so do calm down, my friend, everything in its time."

"Do you think I am hallucinating? The day I saw Umm Hassan . . . Saadiyyah . . . my life became a book named Saadiyyah. A mathematical problem that will be solved only by a theorem named Saadiyyah. Saadiyyah and I will become congruent triangles!" For Ali, this was poetry.

He returned home determined to marry her. He took his mother by the hand. "Do you remember the night I asked you about Umm Hassan's name?"

"How could I forget that?"

"Since then I've been thinking and thinking. Saadiyyah has filled my heart and my life, and there is nothing else in my mind." His mother frowned in surprise, but Ali rushed on, "I have decided to put an end to this life of loneliness, and to marry Saadiyyah."

His mother stood up and drew away from him. "Loneliness, is it? And to get married, and to Umm Hassan? What a poor, naughty boy! You want to marry a widow, a mother of two grown children? Are you mad? Is the world finished? Has Mecca no other women but Umm Hassan? If you really want to marry, I will choose a girl for you. Umm Hassan indeed!"

Her words fell like stones upon his ears. He ran to his room to bury his hopeless pain alone. The situation did not accommodate discussion, that he knew. and even if it did, she was always victorious. He could not have her angry with him. And he knew that she would forever put off finding him a bride, and even if she finally chose one, he wanted only Saadiyyah.

As soon as he could he escaped to his friend Shaykh Salih, where he cried like an orphaned baby. Shaykh Salih looked at him with pain. "Do you leave your destiny to your mother to exploit? Do you give up your future and your love just to please an old woman?"

"But she would be so angry that Saadiyyah could not live with her, I could not live with her. And she cannot be left all alone. . ."

"Where is your masculinity, your will? Have you no determination?"

Shaykh Salih's words sounded strange to him. How could he fulfill his desire against his mother's orders? "Maybe if I wait, she will change her mind. . ."

"Well, well, maybe so, if Allah wills it," said Shaykh Salih, wondering if he had been too severe with his friend.

When Ali returned home that night he not only found his dinner not ready, but also his clothing and other belongings outside the window of his room. Then his mother's head appeared from another window. "There are your things," she said. "Take them and do not show me your face again. I have dedicated my life to you, and now, when white hair is spreading all over my head and weakness is overtaking my body, you turn against me. I will not have an ungrateful child living with me. Go, go, leave me alone!"

He heard a door slam. He rushed into the house and knelt before her crying, "Oh my mother, I ask your forgiveness, I beg Allah's forgiveness. I did not mean to disobey you. Did I make you angry? I'll forget the whole matter. I will never think again of marriage, not to any woman!" His legs would not stand, so he crawled to his room shivering as if he had a fever. "My mother first, her satisfaction first, before anything else," he murmured into the darkness.

When he greeted Shaykh Salih the next day his face wore the seriousness it had always worn before the Umm Hassan distraction. "We teachers must make sacrifices to others' happiness," he repeated several times.

20

By My Satisfaction With You

by Luqman Yunus

The funeral rituals had just ended and the people had dispersed, silent, walking with heads bowed, repeating the clichés.

People do not usually attend funerals because of the beautiful black eyes of the deceased; they attend out of social obligation to his living relatives, so that none can make accusation of disrespect for social duty. But many, disregarding the grandeur of death, use this practical occasion to chat with friends or pursue business deals. One wonders, if the deceased could watch his friends busying themselves at his funeral with matters of inflation, promotion or investment, what would he say? Would he just nod in pity, or would he shout, "Oh, people, shame on you!"

But those who accompanied the coffin of Abbid Kaffass to his grave were not like this. All walked under true grief. They were few in number, but their silence was heartfelt. They did not cry out "There is no god but Allah!" in a mechanical chant as they carried the coffin.

Abbid, the decesed, had been neither a wealthy benefactor of the poor, nor a relative of an important official with whom people had shared happiness and misery, nor a public star or genius whose death would be a national loss, but merely a young man of twenty-five who had worked as an office clerk.

After the funeral, our evening gathering was quiet. No laughs rose; no one wanted to play the usual games. Each of us sat sadly silent, and our friend Hussein Jabir didn't even eat his usual sunflower seeds, the habit by which our wives and mothers always knew of his presence among us, by the scattered hulls on the chairs and carpets.

We felt the weight of the heavy silence. Suddenly, someone said loudly, "Perhaps the scorpion is happy after killing him. She is the

21

killer, I swear she is. She pushed him through that window."

"Repeat that and seek forgiveness!" said Hussein Jabir who, being saddest of all, tried to create a facetious atmosphere. But silence prevailed.

"He used to obey her blindly, may Allah forgive him," said Muhammed.

"With your permission," I excused myself, "I must go home, to try again to sleep a little." I had spent the whole night awake with the terrible scene before my eyes: Abbid lying in his blood and brains, his body totally broken by his sudden fall from the top floor of their house, while his mother's shouts and cries echoed endlessly in my ears. "May Allah refuse mercy to those women who ruined him! May Allah punish them in Hell! May the devil be their companion!"

Now, added to the echo, was my friend's "The scorpion is the killer, I swear she is. She pushed him..."

***

Abbid, when we first knew him, was a docile and industrious student, though not an outstanding one. He never indulged in our playful mischief, which made him something of a teacher's pet, though no teacher would have wished to have a child of his own like Abbid. When we dreamed of our futures, one of us wanted to be a surgeon, another to be a successful merchant, another a teacher to educate the coming generation; but most of us chose political economy. None of us knew what that was, but it was a new field that sounded seductive. Abbid, though, would not state his ambition. His silence both upset and attracted us, and we would tease and taunt him. He faced our torment so patiently that we called him "sissy" and "lady boy."

Abbid was an only child whose father had died in his infancy. His mother refused to remarry, claiming, "There is nobody for me now but my dear son," and she protected him passionately. She wouldn't let him play in the streets, or stay out past eight, for it was too dangerous; she wouldn't let him play with "naughty boys," for they were a bad influence. By "naughty boys," of course, she meant us. In fact, Abbid didn't know how to play at all. He grew up a timid and docile boy who watched from his window as we ran about discovering new rough games, or playing soccer or *kabat*. He watched us with expressionless eyes, eating nuts and sipping green tea.

One day we had news that was the center of our discussion and satire all day. Abbid had finished his studies and started work as a clerk in a government office. Strangely, all of us envied him: most of us were older than Abbid, yet he had been freed of school and become a man before us. We would see him maturely walking to his office or coming back, wearing a black coat and carrying a black umbrella. He became less reserved in this new status, which made us feel like children, and we treated him with respect.

I knew him better than most, for he lived in my neighborhood, and I often visited his home—motivated, I admit, by the delicious nuts and green tea. One day he told me, "My mother wants me to marry. What do you think?"

What could I say? He was too young, but I knew the strength of his mother's influence. She was sure that she knew best what was and wasn't good for him. If he hesitated, she had only to add, "By my satisfaction with you as your mother!" to her orders, and he would obey.

So Abbid was the first of us to marry, and I thought my friend would "live happily ever after," as the old tales say. But a few months afterward he visited me. He was pale as an invalid, and fell into the cushions by my side.

"What's the matter?" I asked.

He sighed deeply and said, "My mother wants me to divorce my wife. She has discovered many defects in her. What should I do?"

What could I say? I knew the "defects" were his mother's weapons, and Abbid would have no resistance. "What defects?" I asked.

"She doesn't like the way my wife does things. And she says she is lazy about doing them. I don't know, it's all household matters that I don't know about. I'm not there all day." Certainly it was his mother's household, not his wife's. "She cries a lot," he went on, "and my mother says she has a bad disposition." Abbid couldn't make any judgments without advice, and it was clear that he had moved a bit from his mother's influence toward his wife's. He liked her. Maybe he even loved her, or would have, if he'd had enough independence for so strong a feeling.

I don't remember what I said. I might have asked a prayer for honesty and tact. I couldn't help. Abbid divorced his wife unpleasantly. "By my satisfaction with you as your mother!" played its usual role to destroy his hesitation.

After a time, Abbid remarried: a widow this time, older than Abbid. She was a friend of his mother's, thus the woman was trying to do two things at once. But after the wedding the friendship changed to animosity, and then to continuous battle. "By my satisfaction..." appeared again to end the second marriage.

"No more marriage for me while my mother lives," Abbid vowed, and I thought that a good decision.

But his mother was restless. "She is afraid Satan will control me if I don't marry again," Abbid joked. "She thinks I have no resistance to temptation." Could the boy who had never had a taste for "naughtiness" really be susceptible? It sounded almost like a compliment, but I said nothing, and it was no surprise when the next wedding feast was announced.

The poor bride had all the qualifications of an ideal wife, in his mother's eyes: a naive orphan girl of vast simplicity, even stupidity, with no relatives to direct her to confrontation, and no charms to occupy Abbid's heart.

A year went by, and another. But the third year witnessed a repetition of the tragedy. The reason this time was new: the girl had not conceived, and his mother was now determined to have a grandchild. "She wants me in her house," he complained, "she wants me alive, but she doesn't want me happy. She tells me how I'm not happy, how no man can be happy until he has a child."

Abbid resisted longer than usual. "By my satisfaction..." was weakening; it took weeks to prevail. But the matter was not ended with his wife's departure. He was fond of her after all, and his heartache added despair to his isolation.

With much difficulty I persuaded him to spend an evening at my home among friends. But even among us, where jokes would make even misery laugh out loud, he was far away. Still, I hoped that he would join us more often, and begin to forget his pain, until one day he asked me, "How can I convince my mother to stop trying to get me married again? No family will accept our proposals now. No one will give me his daughter or sister, for he's sure to receive her soon again as a divorced woman."

"Well, that should solve the problem, then," I said.

But his mother persisted. "What would she do with her time if I were dead?" he wondered.

"It would be some kind of joke on her, wouldn't it?" I said.

One day he asked, "Remember our friend Ahmad? He has agreed to give his sister's hand, but only on the condition that she will not live under the same roof with my mother."

"Will your mother agree to that?"

"What do you think?" Of course, how could the woman accept such an insult? But it redoubled her matchmaking efforts, and her failures redoubled her bullying.

Abbid's depression grew until he could no longer manage his work. The next news of him was both sad and hopeful: he had taken a leave of absence and entered a mental hospital. But he was out again before he was helped, because of his mother's continuous demands. How could anyone know better than she, his mother, what Abbid needed?

And then one morning the whole shocked neighborhood gathered to watch Abbid die in his spreading blood to his mother's shrieking accusations.

"She is the killer, she, the scorpion is the killer!" drummed through my mind. But that was something she would never know.

Abu Rihan, the Water-Carrier

by Ahmad as-Subay'i

We used to see him in the mornings as we climbed up to our school L'Ecole Haute, on Hindi mountain above Mecca. We would see him slowly picking his way under the weight of his big leather waterbag, using his stick as a third leg. He wanted to be different from those who walk on two or four feet.

Sometimes Abu Rihan would arrive before us to the middle of the upward climb. He would have stopped at the place that water-carriers had prepared for their rest, a low wall built to the level of their packs. There they would stand, resting their waterbags on the wall, until they breathed easily again and could continue their ascent to the houses on the mountain.

We were a group of schoolboys whom naughtiness brought together, in those days before water pipes carried water up mountains without human attention, and we loved to cause trouble to Amm Rihan and the other ascending and descending carriers.

Abu Rihan was distinguished by the holes in his leather waterbag. Like a sieve or a sprinkler-head it scattered water on the street behind him, showering the merchandise set in front of the shops and any pedestrians who followed him too closely.

One of our games was to wait for him as he came from the water supply center in the Shamiah neighborhood. We would wait at the foot of the mountain close to some shop that displayed its goods in the street. As he approached, some of us would stand by the wall holding out some *nabq* fruits and yell, "Take this, Abu Rihan!"

Abu Rihan was as greedy as he was simple. When he saw the fruits he would come eagerly, turning toward us at precisely the angle we had strategically calculated, and his sieve would sprinkle the merchandise. We had the most fun when it was something like flour. Then the shop

26

owner would rage against him, and Abu Rihan would realize the joke that we had led him into. But, even as we laughed at him, our fruits would make him forgive what he had suffered from us.

As he continued his ascent, we sometimes grouped behind him, exposing our clean clothes and schoolbooks to his spray. We would push each other until one of us fell between his feet and he lost his balance, shouting a warning. Even then, a small piece of sweet potato put into his mouth as he bent under his load would satisfy him, and he would laugh as he chewed it. He even laughed when we sang,

Amm Rihan, the water man!
We've seen you breaking Ramadan!

He never did break his fast during the holy month, of course, even though he suffered from the weight and heat as he hungered up the mountain all day. But he was as goodhearted as he was greedy and simple. He understood little and cared only to save his money, cent by cent. That was why he appreciated morsels from the children so much—when it was not Ramadan.

Even the simple must have their work and their place, yet often his simplicity strained his customers' patience. If a child bothered him too much, he might throw his stick, and the stick might hit a mirror on display, or a pedestrian, or a shopkeeper, or a child who then ran crying to his mother. Then all insulting names would be hurled at him, followed by complaints to the Ballohlah, the head of the Water Carriers' Guild.

The Water Carriers took pride in their trade. Most of them were slaves, or freed slaves, or sons of slaves.* Rarely there would appear among them some mountain people from the Hejaz region, but they had to carry in aluminum containers. Only the Blacks could carry water in leather bags, the badges of professionalism. The mountain people, whether nomads or villagers, could not join the Guild; and if one of them made a mistake with a customer, the Ballohlah would merely point out his mistake and forbid him to carry water again. But, if a Black such as Abu Rihan aroused complaints, he would be summoned to stand before the Guild Council to hear the accusation and receive the sentence.

Thus, the Guild Council consisted of all those who had the right to carry water in leather bags. Those who used aluminum were not of the brotherhood, whatever their status, and not eligible.

*Slavery was abolished in Saudi Arabia in 1962.

One day, we went to watch the Council meeting to see what would happen when Ahmed's father accused Abu Rihan of insulting his child. Ahmed had sneaked up behind Abu Rihan and tripped him and then danced about him to delay him, until Abu Rihan had thrown his stick at him and yelled *"Kalb! Kalb!"*

We could look down on the Council from the hillside. They met in a circle of ground by the water supply center. The brotherhood had been called by the Ballohlah, and, as they arrived, they arranged themselves around him in descending order by age and status. The old sat on stones, the rest on the ground. In the center of the circle they had spread a *farwah,* and the Head Assistant stood importantly next to it, holding the stick of execution.

The Ballohlah began the meeting with, "This is your brother Abu Rihan" (who stood at the foot of the circle and listened with an expression of resigned misery) "who has committed a mistake against Abu Ahmed. He has called his son insulting names. This Abu Ahmed has come to me to ask his right. What do you see?"

The Council members talked among themselves and finally one of the elders stood up and said: "Please, let us listen to him."

"Him" meant the accused, for the accuser was not obliged to come. He had only to make the accusation.

We soon discovered that, according to the water-carriers' justice the accuser was always in the right. Even when everyone suspected that the water-carrier had been wronged, he would be found guilty. That was to teach courtesy. For the good of the Guild, the customer was always right.

That was what our fathers explained to us later. What we knew on that day was only that Abu Rihan had called Ahmed a dog, reasonably enough, and we were disappointed to see no real confrontation, no argument. All that happened was that the Council heard Abu Rihan mumble, "Well little boys will have their jokes, but. . ." He seemed to know that the Council would not be satisfied without a whipping. So they called him to the center of the circle, where he laid himself face down on the hide and let the head assistant beat him.

I wished that our teachers had imitated that whipping. It was all affectionate formality. The bamboo whip left no blue bruises such as we received in school. If a child were hit all day with it, it would not have equalled a single blow of the sort our teachers gave us.

There was no kinder whipping. When the assistant had given three strokes on the right buttock, he moved to the left buttock. Abu Rihan didn't react. The whipping was soon over, because their law allowed any passer-by to end it by presenting a green twig or sprig of clover, symbol of forgiveness, to the circle. In compassion for his stupidity and cupidity, someone brought one before the seventh blow.

Every day or two Abu Rihan was invited to such a circle of judgement. An invitation could be issued for the most trivial reason: he might have tripped over someone's goat or entered a house with muddy feet. It made the water-carriers proudly professional.

When I finished school and moved far away to university, I forgot Abu Rihan and our childish cruelty, until one day when I was visiting Ijiad Hospital to visit a sick friend, I heard a commotion at the ambulance entrance. There I saw Abu Rihan carried in on a stretcher and laid on a bed. The Ballohlah and several guild members followed, and I joined them as they clustered around him. He looked frail and gray, and panted as if he had been running up Hindi Mountain. He gasped through a face of horror.

When he saw me among the others he smiled in his pain and begged, "My dear son, please ask them why they brought me here. I did not do anything!"

"This is the hospital, Abu Rihan," I told him. "They will help you." But he was confused, and mumbled his innocence. A nurse waved us out of the room. Outside, I asked the Guild Head what had happened.

"He lived without enjoying life," he said. "He never allowed himself a good morsel of food. All he cared about was collecting his earnings. He had a good savings, too, until yesterday."

"What happened to it?"

"That Walid al-Haram! He invited Abu Rihan to meals until Abu Rihan trusted him, and then he offered to invest his savings. Abu Rihan couldn't resist the idea that his money could make money all by itself, without needing a drop of his sweat. The Walid al-Haram soon had his hands on the life treasure of Abu Rihan, and Abu Rihan was boasting, 'I'm going to be rich!' But the first time he asked for some of the profits the thief pretended he had never received any money. Abu Rihan shouted, and he pleaded, and finally he fought, but the wicked one just threw him out and then disappeared."

"He beat him?"

"Yes, and Abu Rihan continued the beating. We found him running about the street beating himself with his stick and shouting 'Stupid! Stupid! Stupid!' We brought him here, but the beating is not what will kill him."

It was the shock that sent Abu Rihan to the hospital to face the shock of death.

29

The Secret and the Death

by Sharifah Ibrahim Abd al-Muhsin ash-Shamlan

She sat on a rock by the still pond, pressing the clothes on another rock, rinsing one more time, pressing the water out again. One last time, and she dropped them into a deep tray. She wound an old cloth around her tired head, where conflicting images confused her thoughts. She wiped sweat from her forehead and balanced the tray, about to stand up, when a thorn jabbed her left toe. She placed her burden on the rock and knelt to remove it and carelessly throw it aside; she was used to this, for her feet had never known shoes. Again she balanced the tray on her head. Her thin body, the same proportion everywhere but for two small bumps on her chest representing her sex, felt very hot.

She walked in slow, heavy steps, repeating a sad folk song, until some children recognized her voice and began to shout, "The mad woman, the mad woman!"

They threw stones at her and some of them hit the deep tray, making various sounds. "You sons of swine!" she shouted at them. "Am I the mad one, or are your mothers, who let you run to mischief in the streets?"

"You are! You are!" taunted the worst among them.

Nervously she retorted, "A madwoman does not wash clothes. I wash your clothes, I clean your dirt!"

"Because you are mad," the same kind answered her.

As she gestured angrily her skirt fell down, and before it her tray of clean clothes. Enraged, she gathered stones and ran after the loudest child. He ran behind a house, and at the same time a young man in the dirty clothes of a laborer emerged. Her rock caught him on the neck.

"What is the matter, Zahrah?" he asked understandingly.

30

"They are calling me a madwoman, but I am not mad. It's your crazy sister's fault, she spread the rumors! It's all her fault that I am so abused. I'm not mad. I only say what I think!"

"Oh, Fattma wouldn't do that," Hamdan soothed. "She's your brother's wife, practically your sister!"

That's just why she does it, Zahra thought. She is afraid Hamdan might like me! But she was silent, because his words stirred her hope. Even more hope stirred when Hamdan stroked her shoulder kindly and said, "No, Zahra, you're not mad, you're only good-hearted at a time when goodness is considered madness. Who but you feeds hungry dogs? What other woman would speak out in public as you do?

She felt as if heaven had opened up and life had become a festival, with loud singing and beating drums. While he left for his work place on the bus, she ran toward her festivals: in the street she began to dance, and she danced until children gathered to clap a rhythm for her and their mothers came to their doorways to stare. The owner of the spilled clothes shouted, "Oh! My clothes are ruined!" and an old woman asked, "Don't you know that she is mad?" "How unlucky I am," retorted the woman, "that whenever her madness shows I'm the one who takes the loss!"

Zahra fell to her knees, exhausted from the dancing. A little girl had run to her brother Saad to tell what was happening, and Saad and Fattma appeared. They gave her their hands: the warm helping hand of a brother and cold sharp nails of a jealous woman. When they were home, Fattma said bitterly, "It is my fate to live with insanity!" and only a stern reproachful look from Saad stopped her from saying more.

Zahra could complain only to herself; she swallowed her feelings, and her brother and his wife left her alone. Half an hour later she was sobbing. But a person spoke to her that night when she went to the well. It was her secret.

From that day Zahra entered a new era. Daily she went to the pond, washed the clothes, returned to see her love before he left for work, and danced in the street. Even after women refused to give her clothes to wash, she went anyway. When the school year started, she had some rest from the boys' stones and jeers. Saad and Fattma remarked on changes in her, but she did not specify, and they left her alone.

The dusty neighborhood was very quiet the day her love whispered to her to meet him in a lonely place tomorrow, Thursday. Joy sang in her flat chest. She felt the wild drum becoming soft, a low roll, a purring. She did not dance, did not fall to the ground, but went home as

31

happy as a fourteen-year-old girl. She washed her only dress and stole some perfume, lipstick and kohl from her brother's wife. Early Thursday morning, before anyone was awake, she left the house to go to her favorite lonely place. There she sprayed the perfume on her breasts, outlined her eyes in kohl and painted her lips. Her face looked like the painting of a child, where she tried to stay within the lines but her hand moved right and left a little bit, but she felt pretty.

She met her love; the bird in her chest laughed; and Thursday entered her life as a sacred day. She became quiet and no longer danced in the streets, but two nights a week, Thursday and Friday, she no longer slept.

Days passed by, and two things were growing little by little in Zahra's body, in her belly and in her legs. Eveyone noticed the belly. The moustaches and beards of the neighborhood moved to comment. But nobody noticed the swelling legs. The whispers were getting louder—"The mad woman is pregnant!"—and echoing from the village walls and the leaves of the palms. Saad asked her: "Tell me! I know how to behave, I will not mistreat you! Who is the man?" But she was silent for, now that she was pregnant, Hamdan could never marry her. Saad would be obliged to kill her seducer; as her only male relative, this was his only honorable choice. So there could never be a wedding. And even if Hamdan did somehow, miraculously, take her for his second wife (for he was already married), how could she live in the disgrace of his first wife's contempt? But that was her best dream, and it was both miserable and futile.

Zahra could only take refuge in her "madness" and hold her tongue. She would not ruin Hamdan.

One cool day a car appeared in the alley and a door cried open. Zahrah stepped out of the house and into the car as people gathered to watch, among them a woman carrying a child high so it could see. The workers' bus was parked nearby, about to leave, and one man was looking downward. When the car had left in its sad dust cloud, a child called to Hamdan inside the bus: "Father, they took the madwoman away!"

His father looked at him with tears in his eyes. He wished to shout to the whole world, No, she is not mad, she is the wisest and kindest soul in the village! She had protected his name, and his life—while he had deserted her to her mysterious end.

Days passed, and most people forgot the madwoman. Quietly the moustaches and beards, and the women's stories, turned to duller news. Only two people, Saad and Hamdan, remembered Zahra. Her courageous silence left its prints in Hamdan's heart, while Saad searched the eyes of all the village men for the criminal who had abused his poor mad sister.

As *Ed-Al-Adha* came, the rich in the village sacrificed to Allah, and everyone was very happy to eat the meat. That night, the Umdah knocked at the door through which Zahra had left two months before. Saad let him in, with his heart jumping. The Umdah gave him an open envelope, though it was under her name. Her brother read the letter with eyes full of fear. Only after reading it three times did he really know its contents.

Then he sighed deeply. His last hope with his sister was cut. The creeping poison in her legs had taken her life, and her baby lay dead inside her belly. Her secret was buried with her, for she did not want to tell.

A Woman For Sale

by Mahmud Isa al-Mashhadi

One day you might receive an invitation to the wedding party of a relative, friend or neighbor. Or you might be passing by a house whose glittering lights and sounds of drumming and women's *zaghareets* might tempt you to pause a moment, smiling, to congratulate the bride and groom.

I ask you to wait a moment. Hesitate. Do not be too quick to participate in the celebration.

True, it is neighborly and right to participate in others' joy and sorrow; true, you must always be quick to help augment the joy of weddings and the grief of burials. But you ought to know which is which.

You are all too likely, if you are not careful, to be partying for the dead and burying the living.

No, you should wait a little. Make sure that you are not about to participate in a crime intolerable to your heart and mind.

On my wedding day, for instance, each of you was racing with the others in helpfulness and joy. Lights, drums, and the feast had misled you to imagine all possible intimate joys for the wedding night. You didn't know that it was the night of the execution of my sentence. Of my heart and youth. The lights and drums and feasting were merely the final ritual accompaniment on a long, dead-end road of loss.

So you buried me to lights and drums and laughter and congratulation, and condemned a living woman to a coffin.

It began---in case you are interested---with birth, like anyone else's, and it will end with death, like anyone else's. We all begin and end the same, or so we are told. But the differences in between! Some are born male, to find all doors opening for them, while others are born female, to find all doors slamming in their faces. Some are born into the joy of

34

good, happy families that take loving care of them, while others are born into the despair of the ignorant poor at the birth of a child. My father resented me from the day that life first flowed in my body, when I was still a fetus protected in my mother's womb. My mother's health was very poor, and it worsened with her pregnancy. She lay in bed suffering from several illnesses—among them her poverty, her inablity to work, and my father's inablity to provide a cure.

The hours of my fight to enter the world were the hours of my mother's fight to give birth and postpone death. My father, too, was fighting—to pull the golden ring off my mother's hand, so that he could bring a physician to relieve her killing pain.

But my mother died in the moment that my eyes saw the light, and my father used the money from her ring to bury her.

So I was a sign of bad luck in my father's eyes, the killer of my mother, the cause of his poverty. And my stepmother, whom he married a year after my birth, never stopped punishing me either, for she was unable to have a child and I was a continuous reminder of her failure to achieve her hope.

All my father had of value was his health and a strong, loud voice. He worked as an auctioneer; he sold other people's goods and received a commission for the sales he accomplished. Our lunch for the day depended on that commission. Once in a while the sale was profitable and we enjoyed a good meal and a full stomach. But when the sales were modest, we ate lentils, or nothing.

My stepmother, too, was in sales, but of a different sort. She was a matchmaker. She circulated through the neighborhoods looking for men who wished to marry but didn't know enough families. Her task was to guide them to girls or women who suited their stipulations. The deal settled, my stepmother would receive her commission, and that commission was all she cared about. Often, the marriage partners would not know the reality until the shocking night of the wedding, when they faced each other for the first time and found that their stipulations had been ignored. Then her client had no recourse but to raise his hands to the sky to ask Allah to pour all punishments upon my stepmother's head. Often I thought He responded; after all, she complained enough about her husband and her poverty and her many hungers. And her step-brat.

As I grew older and felt the femininity mushrooming upon my body and the warmth of youth moving inside me, I comforted myself that the hour of my rescue would soon take me from my misery. My dream's knight would knock upon our door to take me away, to marry me, to fly with me to a faraway land to enjoy love, warmth and youth in my dream's love heaven. There would I compensate for every unhappy day. There would I smile, enjoying tender love, and giving tender love. There would I know the true passions that I had only heard of in the love songs, the poems, that described nothing about my family's life.

Such were my dreams of my days and nights. But even as I dreamed, I was aware that somebody else was observing the changes of my body and my face, the life in my eyes. I was observed by hungry eyes that knew neither love nor mercy. To my stepmother, my youth, my growing beauty and my virginity were ore to be mined.

One day she changed, quite abruptly. She parted her lips in smiles that showed her death-colored yellow teeth. She gave me a generous mealtime portion.

Thus the executioner masks the truth from his victim, offering to fulfill his last wish, even as his eye is focused upon the victim's neck to study the best angle for the fatal stroke.

Custom requires executioners to keep secret the exact time of the execution, and to be in all respects humane, but my stepmother did not observe custom. "In two weeks," she told me, "you will be married to Sheikh Abdul Qader Abuldhahab. 10,000 Riyals! It is the best match I have ever made!"

"Is he young?"

"Young enough to enjoy you. Fifty-seven. After all, what twenty-year-old has 10,000 Riyals?"

"Has he been married before? Is he a widower?"

"He's married now, silly girl. His wife has given him three children."

And the youngest of them was thirty-four. Twice my seventeen years. She grinned her yellow grin as she told me.

Such a man did not marry a young virgin to establish a house for his heart to reside in. He did not marry to establish a family. He wanted only young flesh, and, having the means to buy it from a family like mine, he would buy it. He would bring his purchase into his hostile, jealous family and crush her youth.

All my tears, all my arguments, were lost. My stepmother and my father were determined to have his money, and nothing else mattered.

On my wedding night, that you celebrated so enthusiastically, I knelt at his feet, the feet of the man who had bought me. I washed his feet with my tears, asking him in the name of Allah, the merciful, the compassionate, to leave me alone, for I was not a fit match for him!

But he was only angered by the innocent tears that filled the bridal chamber. He listened only to the savage black ghost inside him, and my marriage began with a rape.

And so you buried me, to drumming and lights and women's *zaghareets*. Since then, nothing has happened to make me smile, or love. I am without heart. Every night when you go to bed, and I am forced to the bed of this arrogant foul-breathed skeleton, I sigh in complaint to Allah and to all of you who helped to bury me. Nobody hears but Allah—and He doesn't respond.

Violets

by Ghalib Hamzah Abu al-Faraj

The violets were wilting under the hot August rays. It seemed a more severe August than last year's. Only the tall palms in the garden kept their greenness despite the heavy heat.

He was waiting impatiently among the trees for the return of his daughter. Soha, or Doctor Soha as he liked to call her, had given herself totally to her work since she had earned her M.D. and her specialization. She was a gynecologist at the University Medical Hospital in Jeddah.

He always had worried when she was late, but in the years since his wife's death he had become even more afraid when she was delayed. It was not just because she was his only child, but also because she exerted so much effort for her patients. Such a gentle lady was not supposed to be able to do that.

When he heard the bell he rushed to open the door, not waiting for his servant, to meet her with a smile.

"What are you doing here, Daddy?" she asked him.

"Waiting for your return, as usual."

"But I am twenty-four! You should be confident of my well-being. Often my work keeps me there late."

"Even so, I still will wait, until that day when Samir comes back from his studies and makes you his wife."

Soha took his hand and entered the hallway of the villa. "Believe me, my father, my heart is telling me that I will not be married to that cousin."

Surprised, he turned toward her and asked, "Why do you say that?"

"My heart tells me so. Especially since I was granted my degrees while he failed his studies."

38

"But he loves you."

"He might love me, but I know Samir better than you do. Even if he is my cousin, he is selfish in his thinking and looks at life only through his own perspective."

"But how do you know that?"

"He has shown me himself. He tried many times to talk me out of continuing my studies. We talked a lot about that. He doesn't want an educated wife, a wife with a profession or a dedication outside the home. I told him that I'd wait for him, to fulfill my mother's promise, for you know how much Mother loved his mother. But I also told him that he did not have to keep the promise if he found somebody more suitable for him. Or found himself unable to continue his studies. And now five years have passed and he is still in America, and still doesn't have his M.S. in engineering, and all his friends have come back successfully."

Then she was silent. "And what else?" he asked softly.

"There is another thing that I did not want to mention, but I will. When Thurayya came back from visiting her brother in Houston, she told me that she learned a lot of things about Samir. He became friends with a Swedish student, and everybody there knew their love story. How many months have passed since I or you received any letters from him? Isn't that proof that he has forgotten, or is trying to forget? I'm as loyal as I must be to the promise my mother made to her sister, but I just wish he would get his degree and come back. Alone or with her. I'm not afraid of being at a loss."

"Would you agree if he asked your hand?"

"No," she said emphatically, "not willingly. But we have to put our hearts aside sometimes. At least our society believes in getting used to each other as the way to love. We're not like the Americans and Europeans who choose their own. So I don't worry about Samir. If I worry, it is only about my patients."

She went to her room and he returned to the garden, where the violets were wilting in the sun.

When would his heart be able to relax? He treasured every memory of his years with his daughter, who so reminded him of his wife; he treasured every day of her life in his home now; yet he wanted her to marry. He wanted the promise fulfilled. Yet Samir. . . Ah, but man's life is like a book of blank pages written by the pen of fate in a strangely perfect way that surprises even those who have experienced many years.

His memories gathered in front of him. He tried to get a sense for his place in this world after his wife's death left him with their little daughter whose childhood filled his life as he tried to make her happy.

39

He had helped her to fulfill her goals.

Allah had given him money, a special status that made it his duty to give. Though he had lost the gentle companionship of his wife, he still felt her presence. Her soul lived with him. He had not seen her before their wedding, for tradition did not allow such a premature meeting, but from the moment he saw her he loved her. Everything came according to his desire. He compared the days of his marriage to the present time, when it had become the right of the bride and groom to see each other before the wedding—and even before consenting to marriage. In his day, the mere request was an unforgivable insult to one's parents, to the girl's family, to all involved in making the match, to all propriety.

His brother's marriage to his wife's sister became the crown of their family happiness through which the family lived its most beautiful years, until that time when his wife began to lose her strength and wilt like the violets under the hot August sun. He had tried every way to save her. That last night she had opened her eyes with a smile and begun to talk about her life with him. She spoke of her happiest memories, and of their daughter Soha. She asked him what he would do for her.

"Cherish her. Care for her in every way."

"I'll not ask you not to remarry, for I know that it would be unfair to ask that," she said. "Remarry if you wish, after Soha is old enough to marry. She shouldn't have to suffer a stepmother."

He promised. That was twelve years ago, and he was still at his daughter's side taking loving care of her. He knew that Soha felt the sacrifice of his singleminded devotion to her.

Everybody in the family knew that Soha was for Samir, as they watched them grow up together.

But Soha was very different from Samir. She was brilliant, and a hard worker. She would be one of the great future physicians in Jeddah. Soha was right: Samir was an indifferent student, satisfied to take his time in his studies and to depend on his father's income. He might never be able to take care of a family responsibly. He might never learn to cherish Soha's competence.

If the ideas of the young and the old are always different, he thought, it is not because the facts of life differ from one generation to another, but because of the way the generations view them. Soha looked gentle and spoke gently, but she had a determined mind that knew how to plan her future independently. She had decided not to tie herself to Samir. That was her opinion, and he knew that what Soha decided was not something that could be negotiated. Though she was her father's only child, and perhaps a bit spoiled, she still had an excellent mind that enabled her to differentiate between what was good and what was bad. She had judgment.

When would serentiy come? They said that fathers must live always under tension, always looking for rest. His rest would be in seeing his daughter married, settled. But was there a man who deserved her?

"Of course, Daddy."

He turned and saw Soha standing behind him. "Are you reading my mind?" he asked gently.

Soha laughed and said, "I've been watching you for the last ten minutes, observing your worry and reading every word you whispered to yourself. Many strings draw me toward you. Your thoughts were flying over more than one garden until you arrived to your question. There are many who deserve Soha, and whom she deserves. Your daughter is one who knows how to choose, when she sees that the time is right to choose. So do not be sad, Daddy. Look at my face and realize how good I am! After all, I'm the daughter of a noble man who knows how to plant virtues in his daughter!

She was silent, and her hands reached out to surround him in an embrace that reminded him of his wife, whenever he surprised her with a gift or a compliment. He smiled delightedly and began to sing a children's song, as if Soha were still a baby. Soha played the role of child with him willingly. Then he looked into her face and said, "I think you want to say things that you have not yet said."

She nodded. "It is not yet time to tell you all I want to say, but be sure I will listen to your opinion when it is time. As you know, I am waiting for him whom my mother chose with my consent. When he returns, I shall find myself free of her promise, because I'm sure he won't return alone."

"But how sure are you of what you're saying?"

"Do you know, my father, that I have been happier since I thought I might be released from my mother's promise to her sister. My cousin gave me that happiness without realizing it."

"Is there somebody else, then?"

"Not yet. I'm very busy in my work, and that's the truth. Still, I'm waiting for the knight of my dreams. Do not worry! He will appear at the right time, and the criteria for 'marriageable age' and 'spinster' are changing. I don't have to hurry. I won't stay unmarried forever."

They laughed, and she went to her room to prepare herself to visit a friend. He started at the horizon. It was true that Soha had achieved her professional position, but all professional positions were very small in his eyes. He saw her in her white wedding dress walking among the women guests, and saw a smile of satisfaction appear on her mother's radiant face.

Pity those parents who think that when their children are grown

41

they can relax! he thought. They are very much mistaken, for the problems with one's children only grow bigger as the children grow.

He went to his room and examined his face in the mirror. Wrinkles around his eyes pointed to his years. He sighed and thought deeply of the future. He longed to see grandchildren playing in front of his eyes as Soha had played.

The telephone rang. It was his brother's voice, in tones of chagrin. "Do you believe it? The traitor has come back!"

"Who?"

"My son and yours," his brother said.

"That is happy news! He has returned after a long absence!"

"I wish he hadn't."

"Why?"

"He didn't come alone."

"Who is with him?"

"A woman from America whom he calls his wife—and two children."

"But be happy, Brother!"

"What about the promise between our wives?"

"It is no longer binding, so do not worry."

His brother was very surprised. "Are you not angry, as I am, then?"

"No, and neither is Soha. She already knows everything."

"But why did you and she not tell me?"

"We left that for the right day, and it is today. And now you know everything, so receive your son in joy, and your daughter, and your grandchildren. But tell me. . ."

"What?"

"The most important thing. Did he finish his studies?"

"He says he wants to go on to his Ph.D.," his brother said. "Of that I'm proud."

"Oh. I see that a little differently. One who has taken all these years for the M.S. might not yet be worthy to pursue the Ph.D. without working for a while. But I'm sure you will know what's best."

"Soha and you, will you come over to see us?"

"We shall, but Soha is out right now. When she comes back, we will agree on a time."

"Until then, then!"

He put the receiver down quietly and stared at the horizon. Soha was now free of her mother's promise. She had not insisted on freeing herself, though she did not want to marry him. Fate gives both what one craves and what one dreads; Soha was both wise and fortunate.

He looked at the violets and found that in the evening's cool sea breeze their wilted leaves were reviving.

My Hair Grew Long Again

by Hussah Muhammad At-Tuwayjiri

)ŀ©ى₂ c⁄©ŀ©ى₂ c⁄©ŀ©ى₂ c⁄©ŀ©ى₂ c⁄©ŀ©ى₂ c⁄©ŀ©ى₂ c⁄©ŀ©ى₂ c⁄©ŀ©ى₂ c⁄©ŀ©ى₂ c⁄©

"Do you want anything?" I asked him.

"Are you mad at me?"

"Not yet."

"But you're silent."

"It's better that way." Talking never got us anything—except irritation.

"What do you mean?"

"You do understand."

"No, I don't, and I'm bored with your riddles."

"You never were stupid, you know."

"Stupid? Who said I was?"

"Nobody."

"So, why are you breathless today? Why so silent?"

"Am I?"

"Okay, I'll leave you to your sullen solitude. Goodbye." He shut the door behind him.

"And goodbye." His cigarette was still smoking in the ashtray. He always forgot things when he left the house angrily. Sometimes he forgot important papers and had to come back for them hours later, or send the driver for them, or just manage without them. He had left his newspaper untouched, too. He hadn't read it with his morning tea, because I hadn't prepared his morning tea. I hadn't even offered him any. This was a first. Every morning since our wedding I had served him his tea.

I needed to break the daily routine of my life. I was freezing, fossilizing. My life was grinding down to slow motion, like a song to a drone, a poem to a mumble. I couldn't feel anything any more. I couldn't care. Neither could he. He knew, he must know. Maybe he felt

44

the same way. But I knew why, and he didn't, because he couldn't. It takes a strong man to live with a strong woman, so he didn't want me strong.

It was time for an ending. Life with him had become completely dull. "How was your day?" "Okay. I'm tired." "What's on T.V.?" "The usual." Our lines were predictable and interchangeable. Sometimes we talked about a vacation, or having a child, but there were always reasons why the time wasn't right yet. Reasons. Reasons. Reasons why I shouldn't try to do this or that, or learn this or that, or why I could if I wanted to of course, as long as nothing in the household routine was disturbed, as long as I was sweet and serene and pretty and comforting, as long as I could do it cutely, as long as nothing, nothing changed.

We were different from other couples. We never fought. We just kept silent, and the silence between us grew. He tried sometimes to revive our old intimacy; but he was clumsy and, as I came closer to understanding my anger, I withdrew from his attempts. I didn't want to discuss either the small or big problems with him. I didn't even want a fight. A fight would have relieved the dullness, but a fight is a relationship, a caring, and I didn't care.

He came back in the afternoon, after I had cut my hair. I heard his footsteps in the hall and I didn't go to greet him; I didn't fabricate the customary smile, either. Acting was dead. I had to try to establish my new relationship truthfully: to make up my mind, act on my thought, live in my beliefs.

I felt his steps stop, and heard him calling me. I found no desire to respond, so I didn't. Let it happen, whatever it is, I smiled to myself. It won't be worse than living with a person that you cannot love or trust, a person who keeps you like a valuable pet, who doesn't want you too smart, who caresses and grooms and orders and rewards, who entitles you to no life of your own.

I was lying in one of the lounge chairs at the end of the veranda, staring at the flowering acacia that shaded the garden wall. I could feel his stare hanging at my back, at my hair. I had cut it just below my ears.

He came around to stand in front of me. My eyes dropped to his well-shined shoes; I tried to look upward but I needed more courage to do that. Then I remembered my position of challenge, and I looked into his face. It was surprised, with a blend of sadness.

He took a handful of my hair and asked in a dim voice, "What's this?"

"Nothing. It's my hair." I stood up and gave him my back; I walked into the house without looking back, feeling his steps behind me. I felt

.iis two strong hands holding my shoulders, and when he turned me toward him my bobbed hair stung my face. Our eyes met. He shook me violently, his loud objecting voice demanding, "Why did you do that?"

I shook free and fell into a chair. I couldn't breathe. My hands were fixing my hair; I couldn't prevent them. I expected him to do something stupid, and I closed my eyes and braced myself for a blow across my face, for I knew how much he had loved my hair. Let him do it! I thought. Let him!

Instead I found him kneeling in front of me, looking at me with despair. Then he sat down at the other end of the sofa with his head in his hands. I waited for him to say something, and finally, as if to himself, he said in a low sad voice, "I wish you hadn't done that. You just don't know how beautiful it was."

I moved away from him and challenged, "I'll do whatever I like. I'm fed up with your control. You treat me like a doll. You just want me to show you off, to be pretty and attentive, to make you important, to predict and fulfill your every wish. Well, I'm not satisfied with that! Do you know why I hate myself? Because I've been obeying you without ever having an opinion. But from today, everything is changed. It's not just my hair. I'm going to have my own feelings, my own needs, my own will. I'm going to have an opinion in this house for three days, three days only, and then I'll leave it. I just want to know that I used all my rights."

Then I went into the study, as I do when I am miserable, and he did not follow me. Falling into our old habit, we did not discuss our problems anew.

The night passed with silence between us. He clung to the right side of the bed and I to the left, and we did not touch. In the morning he went to work without his tea and without my goodbye.

All day I planned, made lists, formulated opinions. I invented arguments and rehearsed my speeches. And by evening, it was enough.

I gave up the three days' vengeance. I didn't need them. Life was too short to spend in misery, either taking it or giving it. We have to make our happiness, after all; it's not a gift dropped upon us. When he returned I had left the house.

He tried a few times to tempt me back into humiliation, but I refused. I did what I wanted. I became a teacher. My hair grew long again.

The Assassination of Light at the River's Flow

by Khayriyah Ibrahim as-Saqqaf

The stage on which action began was at 450 Km., where the road is exploded by thorns. The period is between Wednesday, 19.5.1401 and Wednesday 26.5.1401. The event is assassination.

The distance between moves was the bridge between my heart and theirs, between my soul and theirs. As I saw the bridge destroyed, movement collided with empty space.

***

I was dreaming that my holiday would come on a spring-like day, when smiles and laughs, dew, rain, breezes, the flow of water, the murmurings of doves, and all tenderness would converge in meaning and love. . .

Wednesday. How beautiful are Wednesdays, when joy comes to my heart like a bird that has flown for seven days and then landed on my hand. It comes like a legendary or mythical appointment with joy, it kisses me when I am thirsty for tenderness and hungry for a morsel of "I will see my mother and father for the weekend." I will carry my books to them, and my rosy notebooks, and show them all I have learned. That is the meaning of Wednesdays.

I will tell them of my girl friends, Samar from Lebanon, Sahar from Egypt, Aisha from Malaysia, and Khadijah from Pakistan. I will tell them of their lives, their thoughts, and their imaginings that float on the edges of clouds. I will tell about the faces of our teachers, full of their stories and titles, experiences and travels, knowledge and philosophy. I will describe the green vast spaces we imagine, and our small, crowded, beautiful and safe school world surrounded by its four grand walls that separate us from the external world.

Everything outside: that is the name of the big city in which sleep the rich and the poor, the famous and the unknown, and the schools, institutes, hospitals, monuments, and all the attractive shops. Noises come from every corner. We hear its sounds, smell its air and feel its climate along the road between our school and the airport, where we can glimpse its glittering streets from behind our veils. But when we read its newspapers and magazines, we do not find the city's smells. Even television transmits only routine and unimportant things. We prefer to sit down to a cup of warm tea and talk about our teachers' faces and the graffiti on our walls, and about Samar's weekly letters from her fiancé. We do not even listen to the radio unless we want to know the number who have died in some battle or famine, or about the blood that has been shed somewhere since dawn.

But this Wednesday I decided to stay at school to study for the midyear exams. Oh, my mother, your face is illuminated, how I love that face! My eyelashes stand still in respectful love whenever I see you. My mother, your face is a mysterious world. And my father, my dear father. They say that men are strong, but I wish you were stronger in front of my mother. My heart beats. . .

In a moment I was able to push away the notion of despair. I could see my parents in the next holiday, carrying the results of my exams. They would be proud, and forget that I was one whole week late. They would welcome me with kisses, and maybe a bundle of roses—my success gifts.

Still, something mysterious whispered inside me, the familiar and troublesome heartbeats of time, beating fear, caution, expectation, sadness, happiness, laughter, anxiety and contentment all at once. Days are stops, hours are alarms, seconds are reminders. . .—of what?

***

"Raha!" said our dorm supervisor, "You must travel to your parents right away!"

My heart beat like a dove in one's hands. "What happened? Is my father sick?"

"Oh, Raha, do not be fearful, he will be all right." Those were the words I heard or thought I heard as the car sped to the airport. I did not see the city. I had left my room so quickly, grabbing only my black 'aba'ah, that I left my books and notebooks. Even my written secrets lay unfolded in my room.

I imagined my father asleep on the bed. Oh, Allah, please, do not

48

shock me, do not annihiliate me! Would he be able to talk to me? How would I talk to him? Would he know me? Was it a traffic accident? How did he get sick on Wednesday? Or had he been sick for some time, and not told me? Oh, my father, my world that I trust! Who would await me in the airport? In moments I would know everything. We were landing, and time stretched, my steps became heavy, the space between the plane and my home became mountains on my feet.

And then truth committed suicide. Sweat covered my eyelids and forehead and fingers as I stared at him. There he was, my father, standing before me in full health, smiling to me, waiting for me. I had no voice, something whispered deep inside me, a dead body lay between his feet and mine, a silly lie.

Why did she lie? Dare she do that without being asked to? Who would tell her to lie? But then my heart pointed toward the sky to be forgiven for not trusting that faithful supervisor who took me to the plane with fear and love, praying with me for my father's recovery. She believed the story. So who. . .

It was I who needed prayers.

*****

The day passed in the anxiety of the secret of this lie. Silence contained me. My mother's fixed face did not attract my eyes. My father's face contained nothing reassuring. My little brother was busier than usual. My house, the home that I counted the hours to come to, was saturated by cautious silence and suspense. What did they know? What were they hiding? Why the lie?

The fear was merely the announcement of what was coming. In the evening my mother followed close to me and sat down near me, with words in her eyes that did not content me. My father sat near her, and my brother closed his door behind him, turned off the radio and sat down across the room. After some moments of terrible silence my own voice cut its darkness and I begged, "What is wrong? Tell me, get me out of my fears!"

"There is nothing wrong, my daughter, it is a matter that might please you," said my mother warily. My heart pounded to dizziness, there was something inside me. . . "We would like you to agree to marry," she went on. "A man who has asked for your hand before. You wanted more time, more education, and you have had it. We do not see any obstacle now. He will cherish you, and you will be happy."

"Not that rich, old, fat Fahid?"

As I felt the sting of my mother's hand across my cheek I saw that my father's face was red. "You are arrogant! How dare you! We have made a match for you that every girl would envy! He is mature, he likes you, he will give you everything, he will take care of you. How dare you be ungrateful?" my mother was shouting.

"Made it? You made the match already?" I looked at my father, who just nodded, looking hurt, and I remembered how it was last year, when I watched from my window as my uncle brought Fahid to our house, and how he looked at me when I helped serve dinner, and how I had nightmares of lying in his sweaty bed. But what objection could I make, in my inexperience? I knew nothing evil of him. I had only begged for time, hoping that someone young, someone like the legendary Qais of Lila, or Khuthair of Amzah, or someone like the man Samar was going to marry, someone I could plan with, talk with, whose embrace I could long for, would ask for my hand.

"I can't. I can't!"

"What humiliation is this! What nonsense are you learning in that school? What will everyone say?"

"They'll say that you love somebody else," taunted my little brother. "That you've been seeing men. Maybe that you've had an affair."

"Say something to her!" my mother ordered my father.

"Don't you trust us? When we've always wanted only what was best for you, and sent you to school as you wished? When you know how we love you?" He was almost crying.

"And, they'll say that our father can't control his daughter," added my little brother.

"Don't betray us," my father pleaded. "Trust us. Trust us! Agree, go back for your examinations, finish the term, graduate, come back home to your wedding day. Be happy!"

"I can't marry that man!"

"You will," said my mother.

"I will not! Will you force me to death?"

"Death is simpler, if you insist on refusing."

***

I ran to my room, crying. I could hear my brother's door slam, hear my mother yelling her complaints to my father, hear her voice getting louder, and then she was in my room carrying a stick. She beat me until I crumpled on the floor and then she pulled my hair, the hair that she had taken such care of all my childhood, brushing it, shaping it, showing it off to her friends, calling it the waves and ripples of a beautiful deep black river. Sixteen years of her fingerprints were on my hair.

I had thought that she wanted me to be beautiful among my friends. I did not know she was only preparing me for sacrifice, like a herder who fattens and grooms his goat for the sale. Again and again, she pulled my hair. My youth fell between her hands. My nose bled, her hands were wet with my blood, and I screamed in fear of the blood. I remembered the radio's voice as my classmates and I listened, crying, because of the blood of war victims flowing on paved roads under neon lights.

My mother's heart was the heart of a dumb hangman who has killed his feelings to do his job, a stupid hangman more attached to his full pocket than his heart. She was not my mother. This was a devil. She hardly resembled my mother. Was this another plot? The brainwashing they talked about?

The woman pushed me to the floor and left, slamming the door.

***

I cried until the pain and fear solidified. Then I wiped my face, gathered my clothes, and braided a rope of my hair. I tried to tie it around my neck, but it wouldn't strangle. My mother had given me life, she had given me death, but the death came too slowly.

In the next three days I slept once and dreamed I'd had a nightmare, and my supervisor was waking me. . . I woke expecting my supervisor to be calling us, but it was only a sweet dream. No one visited me. I did not eat anything. I lay behind my door thinking of my school, my classmates, my teachers, my secrets in my notebooks, my secret dreams of love, secrets between myself and my pen, myself and the sky. Dreams as big as space—now reduced to nothing but soap foam, bubbles smashed by mother's blows.

Oh, how great you are, Allah! You made my heart, my feelings! No one can own another's heart, you decreed it so! Even if my room is a locked jail, even if my parents are my jailors and my terror, my heart is still alive. My only escape is through Fahid's bed, and I refuse it, refuse it! My heart is still alive!

I heard my father answer the telephone: "Raha is sick, she cannot study for a while, she must travel," he lied. I wished I were deaf, or incapable of feeling. Tell them the truth, I screamed in silence, tell them that Raha is beaten, jailed, torn, bleeding, and half her hair is sleeping on the floor!

I hear the key opening my door. Her face advances toward me. She plants her glare into me. She advances, I focus on her face, I feel that my eyes will explode. I don't know in what wave I drowned.

51

Poor Oh! Chastity

by Muhammad Abd-Allah al-Mulbari

Oh! My mind will break up! It is not just a headache. It is the pressure of thoughts, thoughts like iron fingers pressing on my head. . .

Mona swallowed another aspirin. It was the third, and she would need the fourth, the fifth, the sixth, if these iron fingers didn't let go.

She stared at the pill bottle. Ten tablets would silence this headache forever. Paralyze the pressing iron fingers. Her heartbeats leapt as if there were whips exciting them, like angry violent horses that nothing would calm, nothing but ten tablets of aspirin taken at once.

Life should not be ended in this cowardly way, she thought. Suicide, the denial of the right to live. . .

The right? Flash-words. Life. Laws. Customs. The right to live. The words were cheap, soft, foolish, rigid. They could not save her. Nothing in life could save her from the pressing fingers.

***

Had it been so wrong to dare? Perhaps it wasn't true courage to violate the customs and traditions of society.

But why not? If she didn't violate religion? Or essential princples? After all, what were custom and tradition but bundles of nonsense for the powerful to use against the weak? Like her brother. Her own flesh and blood, who used the bundle to persecute her, to forbid her her rights as a human being.

Since childhood he had owned and wielded that bundle. Her father and mother had given it to him. "Oh! Girl, he is your elder brother! Do not fight with him. You are a naughty girl who does not know what it means to be polite. Oh! Girl! Give your brother the doll he wants. He is older than you. Oh! Girl, do not let your brother cry!"

Thus her brother Hisham possessed and wielded the bundle, the wicked, stupid bundle of custom and tradition, and in the name of custom and tradition her rights were exploited. Even after she reached puberty. Even after her father's death.

Oh! My head will explode! It is not just a headache. It is the pressure of thoughts, thoughts like iron fingers pressing my head...

She moved her hand toward the pill bottle. The fourth tablet might relax her nerves and lull her body to sleep, to forget her thoughts for an hour or two.

But no, she would not sleep. She would not take another yet. She would search for a solution through her burnt-out patience. She begged her eyes, but no tears would come; she had wept for five years. More than twenty young men had asked her brother for her hand in marriage, and he had refused them all.

***

He always refused them diplomatically, as if not refusing them. She was too young, he would tell them, still in the process of orientation to married life. He never failed to find a bland, polite and spurious reason to delay and, by delaying, to refuse.

In the two years of her sixteenth and seventeenth years he refused fifteen suitors. After that the flood of interested young men ebbed, and she was ignored and then forgotten. She lived the worst year that any eighteen-year-old could live: a full woman, beautiful, and alone, living in the house of a brother who lived happily with his wife and children. It was easy for him to be "uninterested," as he always declared, "in the problems of suitors," and in "matchmaking."

Two more years passed in the stifling atmosphere that continuously reminded her of her femininity, and the rights she was denied: her right as a woman to enjoy sexual fulfillment and motherhood. Her brother's wife reminded her by moving about the house, preparing entertainments, bathing and dressing for her husband's return, exchanging long looks and intimate smiles with him. Her brother's children reminded her as they filled the house with tears and laughter and news of their adventures. Her brother's fake polite smile behind which he refused her her rights reminded her.

Three years with no suitors, no escape, no hope. Then Fawzi.

***

It was exctly two years and ten days since Fawzi had come to her brother to ask for her hand. Fawzi. Why did her heart still jump to embrace that name? Why was it electric, magnetic, still?

When Fawzi presented himself that morning to announce his desire to marry her, she could hear him tell Hisham, "I have come to ask the hand of your sister Mona." And then she heard her brother's hypocrisy. "Is there anyone who would not like to be related to you, Mr. Fawzi? You are from a noble family, and in you all the best qualities are fulfilled. Giving my sister's hand to you is my earnest desire, and everybody who knows you will envy me. But I must request that you give me some days to decide, for she is still learning to be oriented toward married life, and. . ."

Then, after her brother shut the door behind Fawzi, he said to his wife, "What a boorish young man! Couldn't he find anyone in his family to ask my sister's hand on his behalf? I'm sure he could have, but what can be said of these new corrupt ideas that control the heads of young people today and make them shapeless? No one should ask for himself. It's against all delicacy, against all custom and tradition. Anyway, who told him that I want Mona to marry? She will not marry as long as she is in my care. I will provide her food and clothes myself. She does not need a husband, especially one like that."

He might have added the truth, Mona thought. Her brother was jealous of Mona's share of the inheritance from their father. He was afraid that, if Mona married, her husband might inherit her share of the income from the *Tawafah*. Hisham wanted to keep it all for himself.

Oh! My head will explode! It is not just a headache. It is the pressure of thoughts, the pressing iron fingers. . .

Her hand searched for the aspirin bottle. She would take the fifth tablet.

No, no, she must not give in to the iron fingers. She must look for an answer. She would so willingly have given all her shares to Hisham if he had let her marry Fawzi!

Oh! Why did her heart beat so quickly, as if it wanted to jump to embrace that name? She gazed into the darkness, concentrating her mind with her eyes. Her mind was as dark as the darkness of her life. The night's darkness was pierced by the glitter of a star, but her darkness had no relief.

She had often thought of talking to Hisham about giving up her share. She knew he would welcome the idea, but every time she considered it she realized that it would not free her. He would take her money and maintain his dominance. Even if she married. Especially if she ever had to return to her family. If she divorced or widowed. She would be worse off: dominated and penniless, therefore even more dominated. Hisham was her only relative, and her fortune was the only

54

relation between them.

She thought of it that day and knew it was no solution. No, there was only one solution: somehow she had to break apart that bundle that her brother exploited, that bundle of custom and tradition. She would destroy it utterly!

She would contrive to meet Fawzi herself. She would explain her feelings toward him and ask him to go to the court to sign the marriage contract, and let custom and tradition go to hell after that! Let people say whatever they wished to say! She would laugh!

She would gather all of her courage to do what was right, instead of what was customary and traditional.

The next morning she put on eye makeup and rouge in the privacy of her dressing room. And perfume. Veiled and unnoticed, she left the house and walked toward Fawzi's house.

As she approached it, she saw him standing in the street talking to some other men. She slowed her pace until he turned and strode up the street. She walked quickly, then, to catch up with him. Nervously she let her shoulder brush against his, and she said, "To the house, Fawzi!"

She turned toward his house, listening for the sound of his sandals as he followed her to his door. There he faced her and asked, "Who are you?"

"Mona," she answered.

"Mona!" He looked appalled. In a hoarse whisper he demanded, "Well, what do you want?"

"I want. . ."

But in her terror she could not continue.

"I know what you want!" He was angry. "But listen, Mona, I am not one of those young men. I wish I had never known you. Just yesterday I asked your brother for your hand. Of course I'll withdraw that stupid request. I'm just glad I found out in time! Poor, oh, Chastity! You're merely an empty, meaningless word, after what I've seen with my eyes! Leave me alone, Slut! I am not one of those. . ."

And before Mona could say anything, he vanished into his house and slammed the door.

***

Two years and ten days ago. Now almost two years and eleven days ago.

Fawzi, Fawzi, I am not a slut!

Maybe one more tablet. . .

55

Rite of Passage

by Amin Salim Ruwayhi

)ᕼᏸ᳟ ℯℛᏸᏸ᳟ ℯℛᏸᏸ᳟ ℯℛᏸᏸ᳟ ℯℛᏸᏸ᳟ ℯℛᏸᏸ᳟ ℯℛᏸᏸ᳟ ℯℛᏸᏸ᳟ ℯℛᏸᏸ᳟ ℯᏸꞮ

Shaghah was a Bedouin girl of extraordinary natural beauty. She was tall, with a lithe body and full breasts; no one saw her black eyes without loving them. She was engaged to the handsome Hamdan, her childhood friend and co-shepherd, who was broad-shouldered and full of energy and life, as well as courage, character and hospitality.

Shortly before their wedding, Hamdan was asked to travel to the nearest town for foodstuffs for the tribe. The vast desert witnessed his warm farewell to his fiancée.

After many days, Shaghah began to worry. Every morning she ran several kilometers from the tribal tents and up the nearest mountain, hoping to see her beloved's caravan. One morning, she was rewarded when she saw the caravan on the horizon as a moving black spot. Her anticipation made her heart beat fast and her cheeks blush; pulling her long dress up, she ran like a beautiful gazelle to meet him.

When Hamdan saw her he jumped from his camel's back. She lifted her veil and he saw her lovely face beaded with drops of sweat that looked like pearls on her face. She embraced him breathlessly and said in a trembling voice, "Thanks be to God for your safe return!"

"Why did you trouble yourself, my love?" he said.

"O, my love Hamdan, you've been so long, and I was so eager to see you, to be the first to meet your eyes!"

"I swear that my eyes could not sleep but for short moments," he said tenderly. "Your figure never left my mind. I finished my task as fast as possible to return to enjoy looking at you. I bought you some presents. I hope you will like them."

"You are my present, Hamdan," she said. The caravan was far

56

ahead of them now. She rode behind him on the camel, holding him tightly, and he was happy in her embrace.

As soon as Hamdan delivered his purchases, the wedding feasts began. The girls danced with swords, the men fired guns, and the wedding ended in everybody's joy.

Shaghah and Hamdan were the happiest of couples, and their happiness increased when Shaghah became pregnant. She gave birth to a beautiful baby boy who looked like his father. They named him Sattam and raised him as Bedouins raise their children—to be a strong, pious boy full of courage and dignity.

On Sattam's fourteenth birthday, Hamdan began to plan Sattam's circumcision. Shaghah's heart beat in anxiety, for she knew the cruelty of the operation. Many tribes had already given up the ceremony of ordeal. Men must, of course, be circumcised—that was Allah's law—but it could be done in a hospital, without pain, and without risk of infection. She had heard how easily it was done in the cities.

"What's wrong? Why don't you answer my question?" Hamdan was asking her. "Why is a sad sign drawn on your face? The day of circumcision is the greatest day of boyhood!"

She controlled herself. "You're right, of course," she said, "but we needn't do it right away." She used all the weapons of women and pleaded in her most feminine voice, "By my God and my love, I beg you to forget about this matter for a little while." She had to find a way to persuade him to take Sattam to the city.

But she could not find a persuasive way, and a year went by. Hamdan began again to plan the circumcision, and Shaghah had to give her reasons.

"I fear it," she told him. "Remember how Hamad's son died from it? If I have a high place in your heart, I beg you— let us take Sattam to the city to have it done in a hospital, without suffering. . ."

But as she spoke Hamdan's complexion changed, and he jumped from his seat and struck her across the face with a blow that dropped her on the ground. "What!" he shouted, "did I not bear a proper circumcision? Are we cowards? Will you deny Sattam his chance to prove his courage? May Allah curse all cowards!" His rage fed upon itself until he cried, "But for the fear of God, I would not leave you alive! Sattam will be circumcised tonight!"

As evening fell, the savage operation began. The poor mother listened to the voice of her child loudly invoking the names of his ancestors. This was required, and it helped a boy get through it without crying out in his pain. If he groaned or cried he would be scorned as a coward, and the tribe's women would not marry him; it would be the ultimate humiliation for him and the ultimate shame upon his family.

Afterward, his mother ran toward him where he was tied down to the ground like an animal. Herbs were plastered upon the wound, and he was released. His clothing was bloodsoaked, his body shaking, his face pale, but he asked eagerly, "I hope I did not shame you, Mother?"

"You were an example of courage, be sure of that," she answered with her tears, and then he had to turn his face to hide his own.

But Sattam did not heal. His penis swelled grotesquely, and stripes of red and blue appeared and grew up his abdomen and down his legs. Fever shook him until he could no longer talk, and by the fourth sunrise he was dead.

"I told you, I told you!" Shaghah shrieked.

"Don't be idiotic," said Hamdan. "It was kismet, it was his fate. Every man you see around you was circumcised just so, and so were all our ancestors, so how could it be the ceremony? When a man's fate decrees his death, he must die. At least Sattam died a man. With dignity. If we had listened to you, he would have died shamefully in some distant city. You would have bought shame upon us all."

The burial was like any other, but Hamdan did not stand with Shaghah.

Later, when she took to running from tent to tent laughing and crying and calling "Sattam! Oh, Sattam!" for hours at a time, they all said, "Poor weak woman, she cannot accept the will of Allah."

Homecoming

by Ibrahim An-Nasir

The road ahead of him was long, dull, winding and pocked with holes scoured by the rain that decayed the mud walls of the houses that had once been beautiful. Its face was rutted like an old man's face, and time had left upon it all its dusty memories. How dear to him this road was, how many dreams and secrets he had told it!

Ahmed's heart leaped in his chest like a caged wild bird. He felt like a knight returning home from the long wars with the sweat of life dried on his face, returning victorious. Yet he felt a strangeness in his excitement, too, something unfamiliar and unexpected. Perhaps he had suffered too much to fulfill his dreams.

Actually, his dreams had never exceeded marrying Khalidah, his childhood neighbor and his love. Would he find her as he had dreamed of her these eight years? Her soft body would have filled out. Her smile would still lighten not only the darkness of his soul, but the whole universe. She was the full moon showing herself from behind the black clouds.

She used to wait for him, each morning, as he left his home. She would sit behind the door, and peep around it to give him her beautiful smile. He loved her golden hair in its two pony tails tied with red yarn, her beautiful dark eyes that looked at him in tender love covered with shyness. When he returned her gaze with his thirst for love, she would run to hide. During his days he would find excuses, errands, that would take him home to see if she were there, hoping for another of those loving smiles, which became a necessity of life itself.

No one in the village could afford her dowry. She was the daughter of Abu Surayh, who would set a high bride-price in his pride, especially since his son Masud had gone away to the oil fields and become rich.

59

How would he find his father? Would he still walk with his thick cane, making the stones jump to the sides of the path as he struck the earth with every step on his way to the bazaar? Did he remember how that stick had bruised and cut his son's flesh? Ahmed remembered those blows as if they were engraved on his legs. In those days his name was only "Ox" or "Donkey" in his father's mouth. But in the last few years he had become "My dear son Ahmed" in his father's letters. Had this ox or donkey suddenly become dear to his father, or was it the money he sent home? Or—may Allah forgive you, Father—had his father been mellowed by some suffering or crisis?

Would he find his aunt sitting on the old mat, with her big smile of tender love? Had eight years further sharpened her long tongue that so often boiled her brother whenever she defied him? How he loved this spinster aunt—for without her, how could he have lived with his father after his mother's death? He wished he could remember his mother's features. But why did he let his thoughts mar his return? Let yourself be content with your aunt, he told himself, and thank Allah who provided you with this other mother who waited on you with love.

She had often defied his father on his behalf. Whenever his father mentioned his desire to remarry, too, she had defied him: "You should live for your child only!" (What child? The donkey?) Was it not expected of his aunt to let him marry, as any man would? But she would not have it so. Maybe now he could understand their conflict, could help resolve it, could repay her a bit.

Once, the donkey had summoned the courage to ask the question that overwhelmed him.

"Father. . ." But his tongue could not finish.

"What do you want?"

Then he had blushed and bowed his head, burning a hole in the carpet with his lost look, and said whisperingly: "My father . . . I want. . .I want to marry."

His father's loud laugh had shaken him and his legs trembled. "Marry, then!" his father had taunted. "But where will you get the money? Or do you want me to buy you a wife and support your wife and children all my life, you. . .ox?" Even in his terror and shame, Ahmed had smiled bitterly at his father's hesitation between "donkey" and "ox." Yet it was normal enough for a father to help his son get married—for any father.

"No, my father, I was planning to work, to travel. I want to go to the Eastern District. Abu Surayh let Masud go. . ." He was about to add that he wanted to marry Abu Surayh's daughter, but he could not find the courage to express his desire. Too well he knew the results of his tongue's mistakes. There would be a better time.

60

He had retreated, carrying his failure with him, and his father's taunt: "Show me, then, what a donkey can do!"

Eight years. Another world, a new world he had never dreamed of, nor would anyone in his village believe what he could tell. What if he told of thousands of foreign women walking naked but for transparent dresses, showing more than they hid of beautiful legs, broad backs, ivory breasts, walking through the city streets exhibiting their femininity that blew fire in men thirsty like himself? Who would believe the buildings that touched the sky, the meat and vegetables in sealed metal cans, the television and movie screens on which the strangenesses of life, the secrets of the universe, appeared? If he described such things, he would not be safe to live in his old home. Eight years!

Khalidah. What a big name; he even envied his lips their utterance of that beautiful name. His loving heart moved like a six-month baby in its mother's belly. His thoughts flew like ghosts leaving their lamps, to imagine their wedding night. How he had wanted to return home sooner, so that his bird love would not be hunted by someone else! But he had to build the stage for their future, for the morning smiles in each other's arms, not just around a door.

Eight years. He remembered the train wreck that almost took his life, and the fire that had blown the oil well as they were repairing the pump, spraying them with oil that attracted fire as flame attracts moths. These accidents had happened in the beginning, when he was still green. He thought of the communities of work: the friendships with men of many tribes and backgrounds, quickly developed through shared work and risk, and firm as lifetime village friendships— as long as the work community lasted—and then as quickly forgotten when someone moved away. He hadn't even seen Masud for a year.

Later he had been transferred to the mechanic shop, where he had shown talent and dependability that his superiors valued in the shape of certificates and increased salaries. He was proud of that. In the oil fields men took more pride in their skills than their tribes—a different kind of dignity.

The 5,000 Riyals he had sent to his father might have eased the conflict between his father and his aunt. He hoped so. Perhaps his father was even saving some of it for Ahmed's marriage. And now he felt no fear of announcing his desire to marry Khalidah.

"Who is knocking?"

"I'm. . .Ahmed!"

The door opened a little way, revealing a face that looked familiar. He should know her. . .she resembled Khalidah. . .Oh! Oh, God! He cried inwardly, may Allah curse my fossilized memory! No, it was impossible. Where was the glowing smile? Where was the beauty? The slenderness?

"How are you. . .Khalidah?" He could hardly say her name.

"Thanks be to Allah, I'm fine. Welcome, Ahmed. . ." She opened the door and gestured. Oh! God, what were these new changes that had blown up her waist and filled her face with sadness? Did she know that he had left for her alone, and come back for her alone? Could she have forgotten the agreement, the promise, that he and she had signed with their eyes?

"Is my father here?"

"No. . .There's no one but me in the house."

God's curse on the devil! Why was she in his house alone? Or had he missed the way?

"But tell me—is this not my father's home?"

"Yes, but he isn't here. You may come in."

Alone by herself? What a strange puzzle! "Where is my aunt?"

"Your aunt is angry with your father, and is now at a relative's house."

"And you!" he shouted. "What are you doing here alone?"

"I'm in my home," she said. "In my husband's home."

Ahmed's feet moved to the road that had moments before witnessed his memories dancing before his eyes. It was long, dull, winding, dusty, and pocked with holes.

The Last Poet

by Ahmed Rida Huhu

ᵂ ᵉᵏⓄᴴⓈᵂ ᵉᵏⓄᴴⓈᵂ ᵉᵏⓄᴴⓈᵂ ᵉᵏⓄᴴⓈᵂ ᵉᵏⓄᴴⓈᵂ ᵉᵏⓄᴴⓈᵂ ᵉᵏⓄᴴⓈᵂ ᵉᵏⓄᴴⓈᵂ ᵉᵏⓄᴴⓈ

"Ibrahim! Ibrahim! Where is Ibrahim?" shouted the teacher as he scanned the class.

"I saw him in the library, oh Teacher, a moment ago," a student answered.

"Call him, oh, Rashad."

Rashad left to find his friend and after a while returned with the chagrined Ibrahim, who hadn't noticed the school bell.

"Where were you, Ibrahim?" the teacher asked.

Ibrahim rubbed his nose nervously with the top of his finger, lowered his head in shyness, and answered, "In the library, oh Teacher."

"Of course. Naturally. And in the literature section, as usual, reading those old useless Arabic classics that nobody reads today!" Then he smiled, and added: "Be satisfied, now, for Allah has comforted you. The Division of Arts and Humanities that you want to be admitted to is being closed."

Shocked, Ibrahim heard himself shouting: "They're closing the Division of Arts and Humanities?"

"Yes, they are, and all the literature classes in the colleges will soon be discontinued. Listen to this!" He took a newspaper from his desk and read: "Due to declining enrollment in Arts and Humanities, which have become useless in the contemporary era, the Ministry of Higher Education has decided to close the Division. Only four students are enrolled at present. Students with interests in literary antiquities can sample them in the high school survey courses. The Division will close its doors as of the beginning of 2071."

The tower of Ibrahim's hopes crumbled before him. Each of its big substantial stones disintegrated into dust. Storms swept his

63

dream garden leaving nothing alive, not a tree or rose. All of the hopes that he had fostered in his heart would die! He would never be an essayist like ar-Rafi'i or a poet like Shawqi. He would never be able to restore life to literature after its present dormancy. He took out his handkerchief and blotted the tears that had smeared his notebook.

His teacher noticed and understood, but pretended he did not see. He hoped that eventually Ibrahim would come to his senses and change his ambition. Literature was, after all, a dead art, as dead as calligraphy and handmade pottery. It was read only in leisure curiosity, and seldom at that. It was certainly not a profession. He had told Ibrahim once: "Suppose you specialized in literature and became Az Zahbawi and Zaki Mubarak together. What would you want people to do with you? Your poems would neither fly an airplane, nor fire a missile, nor design a robot, nor control the weather. Do you want to waste your whole education to become a low-ranking clerk in a shop?"

But good advice was fruitless. Actually, it made the stubborn Ibrahim become a more avid reader. He wanted to bring life back into literature, he insisted.

Once literature has taken over a person's imagination it fixes its fingers in his hair and never loosens its grip until he is dead. Perniciously, the teacher thought.

Thus, we find that poets hold their convictions so strongly that they will sacrifice everything for them. How, then, could anyone expect Ibrahim to deviate from his way? No, Ibrahim knew he would never deviate. He would pursue literature, literature alone, despite all obstacles. He would study it and write it until his last breath. Perhaps he would even restore the Arts and Humanities to his culture and schools. Perhaps he would even become the Director of the restored faculty and curriculum.

He took satisfaction in that plan and decided that he would not study in any other department of the university. If the university wouldn't offer literature, he would study it at home. He kept this to himself in order to surprise people, later on, with the pearls of his prose and poetry. He had enough inheritance to live on for, say, fifteen years; he had fifteen years to restore literature to his country. After that he would be able to make his living at it.

It was a great poem. It was heavy with meaning, suggestion, implication. Its descriptions, its metaphors, its ironies, its music, its passion would awaken those dead hearts that had buried themselves in materialism. When it was published, people would drop their sterile tools and business papers. They would read with delight, and recite, and run to the countryside to experience the scenes that he had described. They would try to describe the values they perceived in his words, but would be at a loss—they had neglected literature for so long—the beauty of his poem was indescribable.

Then they would attack the Division of Arts and Humanities, and break its locks. They would fill all of its classrooms, demanding to learn. And then the Ministry of Education would come to him in a delegation, in a great parade, to ask him to take over the leadership of the new literary movement.

Thus Ibrahim dreamed.

To which newspaper should he take it? The mastheads of newspapers and magazines passed in front of his eyes as if on film. *The Scientific Monitor. The Miracle of the Age. Oriental Industry. The Eastern Politician. Invention.* There wasn't one title that had any relevance to his subject or his style. At last he chose *The Miracle of the Age;* wasn't his poem a miracle of his generation, after all? He took his manuscript to the newspaper office and asked for the Managing Editor.

"This is a poem that I would like to have published in your fine journal," he said gently. "I hope that your magazine will lead the way in opening up a new era for this dying art!"

The editor took the manuscript, gave it a cursory glance, counted its lines, and said, "Two pounds for your quarter-page advertisement, for one time only."

"Two pounds? Advertisement? What do you mean, Sir?"

"Don't you have a hotel or restaurant in some rural area that you want to advertise? I must tell you, though, that we cannot publish your ad in this very reactionary style. We'll have to correct some of it, edit it."

Our poet was shocked and could not say a word. His lyric poem, his ten years of days and nights of writing, "unsuitable" except as an advertisement for rural business? *Allahu Akbar!* How savage were these people? Only ten years ago had literary education been cancelled, and already it was entirely forgotten!

Ibrahim went from one editorial office to another to present his poem for publication. He left each with the nausea of failure. The reaction of every editor was the same: "Sorry, sir, but our newspaper does not deal in this sort of thing."

In desperation, he went back to the first editor. He would publish his poem for money, and await the results. The editor would soon run after him begging for more poems! Then he would win revenge upon the times! Revenge not only for himself, but for all stifled fellow-poets, dead and alive. For Imru al-Qays, for al-Mutanabbi, for al-Ma'arri, for as-Sayyab, for Shawqi.

He submitted his poem and his money.

Two days later his poem was published. It appeared obscurely on the inside back cover. But only the first few lines of the poem were there. The rest was replaced with,

> Visit Mr. Ibrahim's rural hotel.
> You will enjoy the landscaping.
> Beautiful scenes like these.

What a devastating perversion of his art! It was unspeakable! It was fraudulent! It was wicked!

Yet Ibrahim did not give up. He continued to buy space for his works. He attempted public readings, but few people came; he attempted to introduce literary matters in discussion groups, but it was impossible to keep the discussions from returning to economics and politics.

Did his articles, poems and readings have any effect on this materialistic society? Nowhere did he observe any echo of his literary efforts. No letters to the editor, no comments from anyone. He could find no reaction to his insistent call, not even criticism. The world around him was too busy for the arts.

His financial resources dried up until he owned only a few pennies. Daily, his landlord threatened to evict him if he didn't pay his rent. The winter rains were coming; would his old worn clothes protect him? He considered his situation. He paraded his long miserable life, from its beginnings to its present circumstances, through his mind, and he wept warm tears of despair.

But even as he wept, he heard a voice shouting from the bottom of his mind.

"Work! Work!"

It was the voice of hope that never dies except with man's death.

"Yes!" Ibrahim shouted back. "Yes! I must work more. I must succeed!"

But despair, too, has its voice. Into his face despair shouted, "Poor, oh! Ibrahim! What have you to do with success? It is far beyond you. It is easier to ascend to Jupiter than to get a hundred persons to listen to your stupid call. You did not smell the fragrance of success when you had money and comfort; how can you succeed today, in your shabby poverty and hunger? By Allah, you really are a miserable creature. Oh! Allah, help this wretch! There is nobody for Ibrahim but Allah! He has become unique in all the world for his stupidity!"

Ibrahim watched himself suffer a while, observing carefully. Then he took out his pen and began to record his misery in his notebook. He found, in his defeat, rich resources for his new poem. Its title would be "Between Hope and Despair."

Sa'id, the Searcher

by Hijab Yahya Muza al-Hazimi

)ŀ⊚↭ ↭⊚ŀ⊚↭ ↭⊚ŀ⊚↭ ↭⊚ŀ⊚↭ ↭⊚ŀ⊚↭ ↭⊚ŀ⊚↭ ↭⊚ŀ⊚↭ ↭⊚ŀ⊚↭ ↭⊚ŀ⊚↭ ↭⊚ŀ

I find you surprised by my decision, my friend. Let me clarify.

I was fed up with this life of the city in which everything is a ritual without meaning: people's talking, singing, fighting, everything. All the human faces look alike here, even if they come from many tribes and nations—all reflect their dull acquiescence to this dull life that is like a stagnant pond.

You find them satisfied? No, no, the loneliness of the crowded emptiness surrounds them. I see it, even if they do not. And this is what puzzled me until it obsessed me: why did I, only I, feel so alienated? What realities did I long to escape from, or escape to? Why was I sick of everything—people's society, my childhood playground, even my relatives, even myself? Every bend of my life's road taunted me with meaninglessness.

At last I decided to travel, to leave the prison of my malaise for a while. At the very least, the novelty would amuse me. But maybe, *inshallah*, my journey would become a successful quest—for what, I didn't know—a place, perhaps, where my soul could relax.

I hardly knew how to pack, for I began my journey without specifying either duration or direction. I entrusted my automobile dealership to my manager and said my goodbyes to my family and friends, hoping that my unspecified destination would seem to them secretly planned and mysterious, rather than impulsive and ignorant.

I left my birthplace smiling, with none of the sadness that one is supposed to feel when departing from homeland, birthplace, kin and childhood memories. I felt elated, and uneasy about my elation.

At first I hired a car and directed the driver to take me into the mountains, to the end of the road. From there I would walk.

68

By afternoon the road had indeed ended, and the walking under the trees in the beauty of the hills was cool and pleasant. I walked on and on in the silent dusk, and presently the shining moon added its beauty to the serenity of the place.

After topping a wooded ridge I looked into a wide fertile valley. Down the valley I saw a chain of small hills, like dunes, and I ran straight down the mountain hoping to find behind them a village that would give me refuge.

Then I saw that these were not hills at all, but a camp of nomads. I remembered all I had heard about the nomads' uncivilized savagery, and the harsh ways they sometimes dealt with strangers. Well, they would be asleep at this late hour, I thought. But questions rose inside me: how did these people live? Did these poor people know a way to happiness?

I came upon a large herd of camels, and beyond them, even more sheep, resting between me and the tents. As I approached I saw a young man lying on a rug near the camels, his head pillowed on a saddle; he was watching me. His expression showed me nothing in the moonlight.

"Salam aleikum," I ventured.

He rose to return the greeting.

"Aleikum es salam," he said in a harsh accent. Then he began to question me. Who was I, and what tribe did I belong to? Where did I want to go? Why? His manner was serious and unhurried; after each exchange he thought before proceeding. I was hesitant. We see thousands of people every day in the city, and we do not intrude into their lives with personal questions. But finally I answered him frankly, every question but the first, as I realized that his questions expressed sincere care. He wanted to know everything about me to offer me protection. The first candle of my happiness had been lit.

Then he asked again, "Who are you?" I had decided to change my name from Sa'id, "Happy," to Al-Bahth a'n As Saadah, "Searcher for Happiness." But I felt compelled to tell him—"Sa'id." Then he welcomed me warmly and beckoned me to follow him.

I slept soundly in his tent. Just before daybreak, I woke to the voices of birds, of sheep and camels, and people tending them. I could hear someone urging the camel that winched the goatskin pail from the deep well. Then one man after another came to my host's tent to see me, and each asked if he might be permitted to house me for a day, according to their custom. All repeated phrases of welcome as if they had known me from before.

After dawn prayers and a breakfast of dates, bread and honey, I was invited to the Sheik's tent for the *majlis*, where we sipped the bitter

69

green coffee out of tiny cups while the Sheikh considered every problem and petition. Each man's opinion was sought before the voting, while the boys listened respectfully, learning how honor can be satisfied and mercy bestowed. Here nothing was merely business, merely expedient: every gesture was ceremony, infused with thoughtfulness and meaning. There was time, time for dignity. Nothing was trivialized.

At closure, when the censer was passed and each of us had breathed its fragrance, each greeted each once again—"Salaam aleikum," "Aleikum es-salaam"—and we went out past the falcons tethered in the shade on the north side to do the day's work.

And so I spent the next days with them. These nomads were sincere in welcoming me, and their hospitality was not limited by the three days that their tradition required. I learned how it is that they require no police, no jails, no courts. "We are the heirs of glory," the Bedu say.

No, my friend, it isn't just their wishful thinking or ignorant tradition. They know something about our city life. They come to towns to trade. Some of them have tried the life of farming or the life of commerce, and have returned to the tents. "Houses foster meanness," they say. "Tents foster nobility." They are not deluded by the city's attractive glittering facades. Their free simplicity is the essence of their happiness. You can read it from their smiles and the dignity of their customs.

I learned to admire their courage, their individuality, their honesty, their pride in their freedom, and their vast knowledge of their environment. Many cannot read, yet for hours at a time, they can entertain one another with memorized poems, songs and tales. They create beauty in everything, down to their saddle blankets and coffeebean bags.

In short, my friend, I learned that happiness is not in the elaborate clothes one wears, or in big well-designed houses to wear them in, or in titles or servants. It is in the purity of the desert, where you will find yourself purified of envy.

I did not expect my search to end so quickly, and so nearby! But yes, it has ended. I decided to remain with them. They want a Q'uranic teacher for their children, and that will be my contribution. I have come back here only to gather my books and say my goodbyes. And I will keep my name—Sa'id.

Tell Us a Story, Abu Auf

by Mohammad Ali ash-Shaykh

—Abu Auf. . . Abu Auf. . . Abu Auf! the neighborhood children shouted, exchanging looks of joy. They would open his city, loot it. . .

But there was nothing to fear from Abu Auf. He hung this phrase upon his public relations, and posted it as a motto for his dealings with the elders.

—Abu Auf. . . Abu Auf. . . Abu Auf. . .

—I want him to tell the story of the flood!

—The one that took him down to the sea? But the story of the Jinns is better!

—My story comes first!

—No, I want mine first!

Abu Auf knelt down, giving the signal for the beginning of the big festival. Hands extended to push him here, there. The children sat about him, to his left, right, in front, behind, making a complex weaving of geometric shapes and sounds of laughs, demands, breaths, all in continuous movement.

—His story of the flood!

—The jinns!

—Mine first!

—No, mine first!

Abu Auf had to stand up, brush the dust off, break his silence and stop the debate. He stood on one foot and moved the curtain of his big black mouth, stretched his big hands, and shouted,

—War is coming!

The children withdrew, scattered, regrouped, and debated.

—I'm the captain!

—No, I'm the captain!

71

—The flood, the sea. . .

—The darkness and the Jinns!

—My story first!

—No, mine first!

The routine steps of passersby planted loneliness in the escaping sun. People's eyes were filled with overburdened fatigue. The bleating of goats spread the layers of night over the mountains.

—War is coming! Emergency is announced! cried Abu Auf.

—What is your name, O Hero?

—Abu Auf the Great!

—Your army?

—All of it escaped!

—Your weapons?

—Doves' feathers!

—O Great Hero, show us how you open gates!

—Like this! And Abu Auf ran and hit his head against a big stone across the street.

—Like this! he shouted again.

The children's laughter mixed in joy.

—Oh! Abu Auf is a devil!

—What a clever storyteller!

—Enough! We want stories!

—The flood and the sea?

—No! The darkness and the jinns!

—Mine first!

—No! Mine!

Abu Auf strode down the street. The children's eyes followed him, and some caught up with him, others passed and led him, others scattered small ideas upon the road. One had to chase his white ram; Fatimah reached her mother and then ran to catch up. When Abu Auf stopped he looked upon his audience and sat down; they surrounded him; he lay down and made a pillow of his hands.

—Please, tell us a story!

—One, two, three. . .

—We beg you, please, Abu Auf! I will kiss your hand, Abu Auf!

—Once upon a time there was a child, Abu Auf began. He was as beautiful as a rose by the canal there. He loved to walk upon the green grass among the palms, where he sang and recited the old songs. He was a wise child, whom people loved; they loved to meet with him and talk with him. In character he was like a man.

Abu Auf fell silent as his mind hid between the first steps of a caravan that has lost its way in the desert. It was surrounded by sandy dunes and it slept in the hands of death.

—Continue the story!

—Please!

—This child once saw a huge white building in a city, and he said to his father: I'll build for you a great building, a white, green, red, yellow building, my father, if you will allow me to go to school! And once he saw an airplane in the sky, and he said to his father: I will build you a a great, and a medium, and a small airplane, my father, if only you will allow me to go to school! But his father answered him: But who will shepherd the goats? Water the crops? The child was hurt, but could do nothing. He sat beneath a tall palm and wept. Again and again he struck its big root in his grief. Then he looked up, up, into the tree and watched its green branches playing and dancing, and he thought and thought, and he wanted to write poetry. . .

Again Abu Auf fell silent. Millions of eyes had been fixed in the great universe, sharp shreds of broken glass had been thrown upon the roads, and floods had washed wishes away, away, into the stomachs of fishes. Darkness of night. . . naked crime of fear. . . results disconnected from causes, causes from results. . . the world was mad, mad, mad!

—Continue the story!

—Please!

—The child walked sadly back home. He could neither build a building, nor make an airplane, nor write poetry. He said to himself: If only I went to school, I would learn so many things, but how can I now? My father objects. If my mother were alive, what might I have done? But she is dead.

The rocks nailed to the mountains awaited the cool breeze; the old oak spread its shadow generously. His eyes swept the space, which touched his dreams and weakened his sleeping tragedy, reviving him. Mad, mad, mad. . .

—The story, Abu Auf!

—Continue the story! Please!

—Yes. His sister called him to eat dinner, but he did not hear her. He was thinking, his ideas running ahead of him like a flood. His sister asked: What is the matter, my brother? She asked again, but he only cried out and left his home quickly to hide his tears, tears as large as raindrops. And days passed by.

Abu Auf's words softened.

—Blood has changed into milk, he murmured. People lack the old vitality. The pearls are still there. there in the bottom of the deep sea. . .but. . .Oh, mad! Mad!

—Finish the story of the boy, Abu Auf!

73

—Please!

—Days passed by, and days passed by, the child was running in the desert. He became a grown-up man, a madman.

—That's not a beautiful story!

—The story of the flood and the sea is better!

—I want to go home.

The mouth of night opened wide and darkness swept over the grass, and a moveless wind touched hearts and wakened loneliness.

—How difficult it is to open safes of treasures! And how much more difficult it is to value them!

—Is that the whole story?

—Can people play in the sea?

—Oh, said Abu Auf, it is a very long story, this story of the boy that was a village that became a mad town. The flood tears security from the land, the sea assaults the drams of fishermen, darkness swallows light and frees the ghosts.

—I want to go home!

—I have homework to do!

—My village was born with me, said Abu Auf. We suckled rain together. I loved it, I slept in its arms and dreamed its long, lovely dreams. My village and I are not attracted by harbors, or frightened by deserts. She is I, I am she. . . How strong am I? These arms are still stout, my feet are like rocks. My village was born with me, we milked rain together. . . How did she outrun me? When did she turn against me?

—I want to go home!

—I want to watch T.V.! Tonight is the last episode of "Days of the Past"!

—And there we have arrived, said Abu Auf.

—Do you love your town? he asked them.

—We want it to be a big city!

—But what does the big city dream of?

—It dreams of huge white and green buildings, and a factory, and a big airport!

—Not poetry?

—Great white and green buildings! And an international airport! And a factory!

—But these are stolen dreams! exclaimed Abu Auf.

—Stolen?

—Yes! They are my dreams!

—Oh, you are really mad! the children cried, and they began to push and kick Abu Auf.

—Go, go! they yelled.

74

Abu Auf felt dizzy. Sharp nails tore his back, a knife cut him, his feet stood on the edge of an abyss, his head was squeezed between rocks. He jumped up shouting, —No! No, I'm not mad, believe me! I'm not mad!

He had squeezed the children's hearts and sprayed them with fear. They shouted out, and people came running: What has happened? Abu Auf, what's the matter with you? Catch him! Calm down, Abu Auf! What's wrong with you?

—I'm not mad!

—But who says that you are?

—What do you want from me? Who are you?

—We're your people, your family!

—But I'm crazy!

People smiled, and the moon lightened the night.

Abu Auf turned his eyes to those about him. He raised his hands (reassured, if they beat him, that he was still alive, still effective to stir minds and hearts), and he smiled.

—Tell us a story, Abu Auf! he mimicked.

The Authors

Fouad Abd al-Hamid Anqawi ("Ali, the Teacher") was born in Makkah in 1936. He has a B.A. from the University of Cairo and a diploma in Public Relations from London in 1970. He published the first sports newspaper in Saudi Arabia in 1960-1964. He has participated in several international conferences; he travels extensively and publishes travel articles and social commentary in newspapers. He has held several government posts, and recently was elected the first president of the Hajj establishment for European and American Hajjis. His books include *There is no Shadow Beneath the Mountain* (novel, 1974) and *Haphazard Days* (short stories, 1982). His philosophy: "The author's abilities to live and penetrate his social environment are fundamental to his reactions to his society and his confrontations with the characters he creates."

Ghalib Hamzah Abu al-Faraj ("The Violets") was born in al-Madinah in 1932. He has a B.A. in Law from the University of Cairo, and is editor-in-chief of *Al-Madinah* newspaper. He began as consulting advisor for Saudi Broadcasting and has been editor-in-chief of *Umm Al-Qura* newspaper, *Radio Magazine*, and *Saudi Newsletter*. He was general director of the Department of Journalism at the Ministry of Information; he has won numerous awards. He writes regularly for newspapers; his books include *I'll Meet You Tomorrow, From My Country, The Big House, Loss, Colored Papers,* and *Love is Not Enough* (collections of short stories); and *Unforgettable Memories, The Red Devils, Beirut was Burned, The Green March, Strangers without Home, Faces Without Makeup, Hearts Fed up with Travelling,* and *The Years of Loss* (novels). Some of these have been translated into English and Japanese. Abu al-Faraj is probably the most productive writer in Saudi Arabia today. "There is nothing new in life," he says, "but what you create."

Hijab ibn Yahya Musa al-Hazimi ("Sa'id the Searcher") was born in 1946 in Dhamd in the southern part of Saudi Arabia. He has a B.A. in Arabic from King Saud University. His cultural activities include writing short fiction and poetry and lecturing in literature; he is headmaster of a high school, and head of a sporting club, as well as an active member of the Jizam Literary Society. His books include *Faces From the Countryside* and *A Poet from my Country* (soon to be published). His philosophy is, "If the countryside is different from what it used to be, let's discover it. . ."

Ahmad Rida Hulu ("The Last Poet") was born in Algeria. He lived for some time in al-Madinah, where he was a leading figure in short fiction. His stories were published in a local newspaper. After Algeria's independence he returned to take a leading position in the literary movement there.

Muhammad Ali Maghribi ("The Bad-Tempered Man") was born in Jeddah in 1914. He was educated in Jeddah and was editor-in-chief of *Saud Al-Hijaz* daily newspaper until the second World War shut it down. Then he worked to write the Quran, and helped establish a Quran publishing house in Makkah. In 1953 he established the trustees of the *Al-Bildad* newspaper. His publications include *Rebirth* (novel, 1944); a novelette, "Al-Ba'ath"; several short stories; and historical works on the Hijaz, such as *Social Life in Hijaz.* "Life taught me not what to do, but what I knew and loved; for only knowledge is the way to perfection, and only love eases hardship."

Mahmud Isa al-Mashhadi ("A Woman for Sale") was born in al-Madinah in 1355. He has a B.A. in Philosophy and Psychology from the American University at Cairo and further graduate studies in Mass Media and Public Relations from Michigan State University. He has worked for ARAMCO and helped plan cultural programs for Dhahran Television; he is now at Petromin. He writes poetry, novels and plays as well as short stories.

Muhammad Abd-Allah al-Mulbari ("Poor, Oh! Chastity") was born in Makkah in 1930. He has a B.A. in Islamic Studies from the Islamic College of India. He has worked as a journalist and is an active member of the Makkah Literary Society. His books include three collections of short stories, *With Luck, Sunburn,* and *The Devil's Killer*; a book about the Prophet's Companions; and a four-volume history of the city of Makkah.

Ibrahim Al-Nasir ("Homecoming") was born in Riyadh in 1932. He finished ninth grade. He has written several plays for Saudi Radio and published numerous short stories in newspapers. His books include *Our Mothers and the Struggle* (short stories, 1960); *Hole in the Dress of Night* (novel, 1961); *A Land Without Rain* (short stories, 1965); *The Ship of Dead Bodies* (novel, 1969); *The Girls' Spring* (short stories, 1977); and *The Virgin* (novel, 1978). "Realism," he says, "is a way of life."

Mohammad Ali Rida Quddus ("Auntie Ruqayyah's News") was born in Makkah in 1948. He has diplomas in Aviation Traffic Engineering and in Journalism. He is secretary of the Jeddah Literary Society, writes programs for the Saudi Radio, and articles for Saudi newspapers. His collections of short stories include *The Point of Weakness* (1979). "Before it is born, the literary narrative is like the sperm thrown inside the vagina of memory. After a while it passes through the stages of creation to take the shape and size allowed by the scope of the creator's memory. . ."

Amin Salim Ruwayhi ("Rite of Passage") was born in Makkah. He is a very prolific journalist with a distinguished satiric style. He has published several collections of short stories, including *The Kind* (1959)

Khayriyah Ibrahim as-Saqqaf ("The Assassination of Light at the River's Flow") was born in Makkah in 1951. She has a B.A. in Arabic from King Saud University, where she now lectures, and an M.A. in Education from the University of Missouri. Her cultural activities include short story and essay writing. Her collection of short stories, *To Sail Towards the Horizon,* was published in 1982. She is the first woman editor in the Kingdom, editing *Ar-Riyadh,* one of the leading newspapers of Saudi Arabia.

Sharifah Ibrahim Abd al-Musin ash-Shamlan ("The Secret and the Death") was born in Zubayr, Iraq, in 1947. She has a B.A. in Journalism from Baghdad University, and often contributes to Saudi Arabian newspapers. She writes short fiction and critical essays.

Muhammad Ali ash-Shaykh ("Tell us a Story, Abu Auf") was born in Khulays near Al-Madinah in 1946. He has a B.A. in History from King Abdulaziz University. He is the head of the literary society in Khulays and writes for the local newspaper. His books include *Mind Is Not Enough* (1982).

Ahmad as-Subay'i ("Abu Rihan, The Water-Carrier") was born in Makkah. He studied in local schools during the Hashimite reign and is a leading literary figure in the Kingdom. He was the first to establish a theater, and literary and daily newspapers and he is the head of several social clubs. His books include *History of Makkah, Auntie Kardjam* (short stories), *The Philosophy of Jinns, Abu Zamil* (a local hero), and *Memories.* "I try to draw the society with its negatives and conflicts, full of life and movement, in its natural colors, without any artificial makeup."

Hussah Muhammad at-Tuwayjiri ("My Hair Grew Long Again") was born in Riyadh in 1380 (1960). She has a B.A. in History from King Saud University. She no longer writes short stories. She is now solely a housewife.

Luqman Yunus ("By My Satisfaction With You") was born in Makkah. He is known as a satirist; his books include *From Makkah with Greetings,* a collection of short stories.

Dr. **Abu Bakr Ahmad Bagader** (who prepared the rough translations), a native Arab, was born in Makkah. He received his Ph.D in Social Sciences from the University of Wisconsin. He has a B.A. in mathematics from the University of Pertroleum and Minerals. He belongs to numerous professional associations and has received numerous honorary degrees. He is a Fellow in the American Academy of Sociological and Political Sciences, and has published widely in scholarly journals, in both Arabic and English, examples of his work being the essay "A Study of the Saudi Family" and *Islam and Sociological Perspectives.* He is currently Chairman of the Department of Sociology, and former Chairman of the Islamic Studies, at King Abdulaziz University, Jeddah.

Ava Molnar Heinrichsdorff (who prepared the final translations) was born in Hungary. She received her M.A. in Teaching and Humanities. A writer, she co-authored the novel, *The Fire Goddess* (Abelard). Her articles have appeared in educational journals, nature magazines, and dance journals. She is also a book reviewer, and editor of novels such as *Love with Paprika* (Harper). Currently, she is Chairman of the English Department, The Colorado Springs School. Despite her demanding schedule, she still finds time to be a consultant in writing, interdisciplinary and experiential education, cross-cultural studies, and ethnic and international folk dance, for universities and various national professional organizations.

Glossary

'Aba'ah: a black overdress worn by women when out of the home

Allahu Akbar: God is Great

Farwah: sheepskin used as a rug

Fava: fava beans are the English equivalent of the Arabian Foul Mondamas, very popular in Egypt, Saudi Arabia and the Sudan

Inshallah: if Allah wills it. Many Muslims consider it impious to make statements or plans about the future without adding inshallah.

Kabab al-miro: an Arab dish of meat balls mixed with grain and fried in cooking oil

Kabat: a traditional game from the western province of Saudi Arabia

Kalb: dog

Kismet: fate

Majlis: court

Manfush: a fried paste made of various grains

Maqliyyah: an Arab vegetarian mixture fried in cooking oil

82

Mutabbaq: A Saudi dish, a pie stuffed with ground meat, eggs, cheese or bananas

Nabiq: nut tree

Ramsham: a wooden facade in front of the window, built on traditional Arabian houses

Riyals: Saudi Arabian currency, $1 equals 3.75 Riyals

Sambusa: an Indian-Arab dish, a triangular pie stuffed with ground meat and fried in cooking oil

Suq: market

Tawafah: the institution of helping pilgrims perform the rituals correctly, by paying a professional host

Thaub: man's long white garment, worn by almost everyone

The Arab calendar: Year number 1 in the Hijra Calendar is the same as 16 July, 622 A.D. The months are 29 or 30 days long, less than the Western calendar by 11 days per year.

Walid al-haram: son of a bitch

Ya Mala'een, Ya Kelab: "You cursed ones, you dogs"

Umm before a woman's name means "Mother of", **Abu** means "father of", **Ibn** means "son of", **Bint** means "daughter of", **Amm** means uncle.